# Heaven's Lost

## Second Edition

By Vanessa Haney

## *Dedication*

You've probably heard this before (especially if you know me personally because I don't shut up about it), but it turns out that writing a book is the easy part. Getting the book into your hands was much more difficult than I ever imagined and required many skills that I don't (or didn't) have. My village includes a crew of patient loved ones and professionals, without whom the residents of Chuparosa would only exist in my mind. Endless thanks go out to Thomas Schroeder for "getting it" instantly and designing a fantastic cover.

Kelly, you are a badass GenX woman and my best friend. Your support and recommendations are priceless, and I love you. Amanda, as far as sisters go, I got lucky. Thank you for reading the first draft and not judging me-at least out loud. Connor, thank you for encouraging me and for helping me keep the GenZ characters in line. Mike, you patiently puzzle over the scenes I shove at you out of order, you understand when I shut the door and write for twelve hours, and how many times have you talked me out of deleting the whole thing? There's nothing I can write that would sufficiently express my love and gratitude.

## *Author's Note*

I was tempted to use this section for a list of content warnings, but I decided against it in the end. Suffice it to say that among these pages you will find witches, angels, demons and monsters. You will also find love and redemption and friendship and heroism. It's a story written for and about grown-ups. A bit of a love letter to the strong women of my often-overlooked Generation X. A nod to the power that women of a certain age are conditioned to believe they no longer possess.

These characters are not perfect people-some are not even people. So rather than warn you off, I invite you for a visit to Chuparosa. There's stormy weather in the forecast, but us desert rats know that we need the rain.

*Also by Vanessa Haney*

Heaven's Watch (Book 2)
Heaven's Call (Book 3)
The Chuparosa Chronicles (Short Stories)
The Devil's Memories (Book 4)

## *Prologue*

It starts with the dust. A gritty haze of dirt, pollen and dampness. Wind comes in bursts. The top layer of soil swirls into the air turning the sky orange and then brown as the sun sets over the mountains. Clouds roll in out of nowhere, low, and gray, bringing their light show with them. What begins as a distant rumbling grows louder and closer by the minute.

As a few giant drops hit the ground, the gusts pick up speed, snapping Palo Verde branches and toppling road signs. A web of lightning crosses the sky with a sharp crack of thunder on its heels and the downpour begins. In a matter of minutes, a river made of rain sweeps down through the mountains, flash flooding the washes and running through the streets of town.

Monsoon storms blow through with violence but are over quickly. There will be downed power lines and a few people standing on top of submerged vehicles while they wait to be rescued. The residents of Chuparosa call it "getting some weather." Like so many Arizona towns, Chuparosa sees about three hundred sunny days a year, so weather of any kind other than sweltering heat is an appreciated event.

Over centuries, flash floods have carved cave-like pockets into the canyon walls. Pockets that made perfect little portals. When settlers built their town at the base of the mountains, the beings that came and went through those portals didn't really mind. Sure, people were an inconvenience, but they'd had a decent relationship with the native humans that came before. Humans occupy one Side of the veil, and the portal dwellers live on the Other Side. It's not especially wise for either to cross the borders, although they aren't always clear.

The families in Chuparosa are old and they've passed down some helpful tips: feed the birds shelled sunflower seeds and they'll stay out of your garden; leave an open jar of lemonade on the porch and your pets will be protected; if you don't want scorpions in your house, you'll keep the hummingbird feeders filled; never, ever, step on a wolf spider if you have a newborn; and, no one really knows why, but don't forget to leave orange slices out for the butterflies. None of this makes any sense and it's all subject to change, but there's no point in borrowing trouble.

In the sixties, archeologists discovered evidence of the indigenous mountain settlements and tourists started to explore. They tore up the landscape in search of petroglyphs and pottery, and some even scored their own carvings in the rocks to try to make a buck.

When developers started sniffing around, the county came in and designated the entire mountain range and surrounding area as a regional park. A dozen hiking trails were established and the delicate ruins that remained were cordoned off or moved to a tiny nature center near the park gates.

The town of Chuparosa remained tucked in the foothills, remarkably unbothered. The area boasts some of the most dangerous black diamond trails in the country and while winter tourists flock to the area for the hiking, they don't tend to linger. The park is roughly fifty miles west of Phoenix, but the town offers no hotels, no campground, and very little else in the way of amenities. This is by design. Come and enjoy the trails and the desert scenery. Then, go away.

Most people don't move away and very few move in. Those who do come to stay are likely running from something, tired of running, or just want to be left alone. Usually some combination of the three. Chuparosa as an entity is quite able to figure out a person's intentions. It doesn't necessarily care what they are, but it knows who belongs and who doesn't.

When the new deputy sheriff arrived, bone weary from a series of bad decisions and bad luck, he might have turned away at the edge of town. In fact, he very nearly did. While sitting at the only traffic light, he scrutinized Main Street. It was typical: a bar, a diner, a school, a library, a gas station, and a small grocery store. Houses were tucked in between the businesses and in uneven rows that backed up to the mountains. There were no kitschy shops, no cowboy art, no cactus jelly carts, and no boutiques. Nothing to draw in strangers. He saw only the locals picking up their kids and running errands. And, of course, there was the heat.

He rested his head on the steering wheel and shifted his body in the seat as sweat ran down his back. He might have retreated that second. Might have, but for the tender little tug on his soul. *Sebastian, what you need is here.*

Those who don't belong can feel it, too. An uneasiness washes over most visitors that they can't quite explain. Every now and then hikers will report something peculiar like sudden dizziness or blurred vision. They might see a three-foot tall jackrabbit or be harassed by a bouquet of angry hummingbirds. The authorities, such as they are, respectfully study the fuzzy photos on the victims' phones and offer them some water.

"You know, you're lucky you didn't pass out from a heatstroke. We wouldn't find you before the mountain lions do. Ha, ha, ha. You've got to be careful out here."

Most outsiders are happy to get back on the outside. That said, it would be a mistake to assume that quiet and privacy equal tranquility. Life in Chuparosa is not perfect and neither are its people. Residents there seem to have an above average share of personal demons, fueled by secrets and shame. One could argue though, that Chuparosa also has a greater share of heroes, fueled by bravery and love. It's just that sometimes it can be hard to tell the difference between the two.

## Chapter One

*1986*
The girls were sprawled in front of the television trying to make sense of a scrambled music video when the fight started. Their parents were arguing about money. It was always about money. Laura and Sarah could assume that their mother hadn't paid the water bill or that she bought the wrong truck part or something equally ridiculous.

Kevin and Brona argued in the kitchen that night, but Laura reached up to turn down the television anyway, so as not to add to the ruckus. Her younger sister, Sarah, had one eye on the screen and one eye on Tiger Beat magazine. The fighting had long ago become their normal background noise. Unlike her sister, Sarah did not care to be quiet and make accommodations for the madness. Instead, she shoved the magazine cover in Laura's face.

"Look at this: Go Swayze Crazy? Gross. I bought this for Rob Lowe, and there's only two good pages on him. What a total waste of babysitting money."

"Shhhh." Laura took the magazine and laid it to the side. Inserting themselves, even inadvertently, into their parents' concerns could get them beaten, or worse, grounded. She found invisibility to be the most efficient means of survival.

An unpaid phone bill was the catalyst that night, though they were using a pretty broad brush. He didn't make much, but Kevin brought home enough money for them to survive on. What Brona hated was that he lost interest after the work was done, leaving her in charge of the bills and everything else. She resented her role as ignored housewife and that it was her job to write checks for things she didn't care about.

To get out from under her mother's thumb, she and Kevin had run off to get married at eighteen, but home economics class did little to realistically prepare the young girl for taking care of a home and children.

Kevin discovered early on that his wife's attitude served him well. He believed his marriage to be a mistake, but also that he would go to Hell if he ended it. Rather than working out why things fell apart every month and how to fix their problems, he hid behind rage and self-righteousness when they invariably did.

The girls jumped when Brona finally exploded. "You hate me! You wish I was dead!"

Sarah cocked her head in their direction, then rolled her eyes at her sister. Laura simply turned away. "You wish I was dead" was *Brona Code* for, "I didn't pay the bill because I hate you, and I hate my life, and I'm acting crazy because that's the only way for me to get attention."

Kevin opened the freezer door and slammed it hard, sending loosely clipped bags of chips and cereal boxes flying off the top of the refrigerator.

So, it was going to be one of *those* fights. Laura turned off the television and the girls sat up straight in front of the couch, wrapping their arms around their shins. Their bedroom was just beyond the kitchen, so their only escape route was blocked. Sarah rested her forehead on her knees and heaved a sigh.

He opened the freezer door again, grabbed a handful of ice and threw it at Brona. She raised her arms defensively and shrieked as scratches from her wrists to her elbows began to bleed, then she lowered her arms, narrowed her eyes, and jerked open a drawer.

Laura knew what was in that drawer and she felt her insides begin to churn. Brona grabbed the revolver, cocked the hammer and put the pistol to her temple.

"I'll do it, I swear! That's exactly what you want isn't it?"

He stepped toward her. "Give it to me, Brona. Don't be so stupid."

She pointed the gun at him. "Stay away from me or I swear I'll do it."

Sarah whimpered and pulled herself tighter into a ball. Laura nudged her younger sister and they flattened onto their bellies, scooting toward the front door. There was nowhere to take cover, but Laura was pretty sure they wouldn't get shot if they could get outside unnoticed.

Kevin was furious. "You're insane!"

Brona moved the barrel under her chin. "Don't call me crazy! If I'm crazy, it's only because of you!"

"Give it to me, please. You know you don't want to do this." He swiped at her, but she ducked his reach and laughed. As if suddenly bored with her own antics and satisfied that he was sufficiently worried, Brona dropped the gun on the kitchen table. She grabbed the keys to the truck and pushed past him, never glancing down at the girls on the floor as she stomped around them on her way out.

Sarah rested her head on the floor, giggling nervously as the stress left her body. "Holy crap."

Shaking his head, Kevin picked up the revolver and released the hammer. He checked the cylinder, clicked it back into place and returned the gun to the drawer. The girls stood up, eyes wild, as he turned and started toward them. His face was drawn and tired and he looked like he might say something to try to comfort them until he stepped on the magazine. Laura stopped breathing as he reached down to pick it up.

"What did I tell you about this trash?" He rolled it up, threw it at her, and pointed behind him to the food scattered across the kitchen floor. "Get in there and clean it up." With that, he went to his bedroom and slammed the door.

As a preemptive strike against further punishment, they decided to clean the whole kitchen. Laura planned to have them safely in their room before Brona came home, but they heard the truck pull in the driveway as they were finishing the dishes. Brona strolled through the kitchen and started making a pot of coffee as if it had been the most casual of evenings.

"Where did you go?" Laura asked.

"None of your business." Brona looked around. "Where did you put those receipts that were on the table?"

"I threw them away, they were just for groceries and stuff."

"Nice job, Sherlock. I needed those." Brona glared at her and dug through the trash. "Go to bed, but make sure you have clean clothes for church tomorrow."

**_Present Day_**

The wailing began as Sarah was folding clothes on the coffee table. They came and went throughout the day; those screams of anguish that only she could hear. There was no way to make it stop until the end and her anxiety was rising by the minute.

"Oh my god Mom, just call Auntie." Her twenty-year-old daughter, Audra, lounged on the couch scrolling social media and glancing occasionally at her anatomy textbook. "There must be some news by now."

Exhausted and on edge, Sarah agreed to call her sister, but her cell phone rang as she reached for it.

"Tell me what's happening." she blurted.

Laura's voice was strained and tired. "We're still at the hospital, but they are moving her to hospice and you should probably come. I'll text you the address."

Sarah pressed the red button to end the call, wishing there was a red button to end the whole nightmare.

A twinge of guilt fluttered in her stomach when she thought of Laura at the hospital by herself, gathering up Brona's things and apologizing to the nurses for their mother's terrible behavior. Navigating the medical system on Brona's behalf was a job neither of her daughters wanted, but Laura had the misfortune of being the oldest, and recently retired.

Brona's terminal cancer diagnosis hadn't come as a surprise. A lifelong smoker, she'd already been battling emphysema and congestive heart failure. What never ceased to amaze her daughters was the expert level manipulation she was able to employ, even as sick as she was. And how they found themselves falling for it every time.

"You don't have a job," Brona had grumbled at Laura, "and don't talk to me about your little 'business'. Making expensive tea isn't work."

"She's already selling in twenty shops, Mom." Sarah defended.

"Are you saying I matter less to you than tea?"

"She didn't say that." Most people wouldn't think twice about helping a sick parent, so guilt chewed at Laura even though she knew exactly how it would go.

Brona made a show of adjusting her oxygen tank, so Laura made a show of emptying the full ashtray. Undeterred, Brona knew that by deploying a little more shame, she could get her way.

"What do you want me to do? Should I just kill myself now? I suppose if I accidentally lit a cigarette too close to the oxygen, it would spare you the tedium of my last few months."

There was no way that Laura, the ever-dutiful first born, wasn't going to help her mother, if for no other reason than to protect the other residents of the building from explosion.

"Relax, Mom. You have to admit though, that this would be easier if we could get along. Can we please do that?"

"You mean it would be easier if you didn't hate me."

Sarah sniffed. "Fair enough."

For that, Sarah had been banned from Brona's bedside for the duration, which suited her just fine, but it made Laura's life much harder.

Once again, the tortured wail surged through Sarah's brain, and she grabbed her purse. "Audi, let's go."


Sarah heard the screams for the first time when she was fifteen. One day before school, what she thought was a whistle woke her a few minutes before the alarm.

"Knock it off," she'd grumbled, and kicked her foot between the slats into the mattress on the top bunk.

Laura leaned over the side of the bed and flung a pillow at her. "What is your damage?"

"Stop whistling!" Sarah hissed.

"I'm sleeping, slut, leave me alone."

"Do you have your Walkman on? What's whistling?"

Laura climbed down the ladder, glared at her, and stomped to the bathroom.

The girls' room was an attachment built on to the house by a previous owner, most likely for an aging parent or in-law. At one time, a side door led outside from the kitchen. That door now led to a bedroom that led to a walk-in closet that led to a bathroom. The bunk beds were flush against one wall and a large chest of drawers sat against the opposite wall. A thrifted, oval-shaped coffee table was cluttered with a small boom box, scattered cassette tapes, banana clips, paper, and markers.

A blank space, outlined in dust, remained on the table from the night before when Kevin took their portable black and white television. It had been a Christmas present from their parents, but he decided watching television alone in his room, even in black and white, was preferable to watching television in the living room with his wife.

The walls were still pink from when they were little, but the teenaged girls had them covered in posters of Duran Duran and Bon Jovi. There was also a movie poster from the Breakfast Club on the wall next to Laura's bed. A heart had been drawn around Judd Nelson with red and silver Outliner pens. On the wall between the bunks, Sarah hung a row of Rob Lowe pictures, carefully culled from her Tiger Beat magazines.

There were no doors between the bedroom, the closet, and the bathroom, so when Sarah heard the shower come on, she got up and went to the bathroom sink. She used her fingers to scoop some Neutrogena from the jar and swirled it onto her cheeks, pausing mid-scrub as the whistling started again. No, not a whistle that time. A...howl?

Her reflection blurred slightly in the mirror, so she blinked several times. Glancing at the shower curtain, she realized at last that her big sister wasn't making the noise, and Laura obviously couldn't hear it, either.

Sarah rinsed the cleanser from her face and peered in the mirror again. The tiny bathroom was shrouded in steam from the shower, yet a light, cool breeze washed over her neck and covered her body in goosebumps.

A slight silhouette, hazy and distorted, gradually appeared behind her in the reflection but no one was there when she spun around. Back in the mirror, the figure opened its mouth, and for a moment, she thought it might speak to her. Instead, it separated its jaws and began to scream. Low at first, but louder and louder by the second. She put her hands over her ears and collapsed.

Laura hadn't heard a thing and when she peeked around the curtain to grab a towel, she found Sarah rocking back and forth on the floor.

They skipped school that day to do some research, combing the card catalog for books about ghosts. Chuparosa's little library didn't have much of a selection and it didn't take them long to get discouraged.

The mirror creature was gone by the time Laura finished her shower, so she'd quizzed Sarah at length. "Was it floating? Was it on fire? Did it have teeth? Did it talk to you?"

"No, no, no, no. It just screamed at me."

That was not the first time they'd experienced something strange. They'd been noticing little oddities about themselves and their surroundings since Laura's twelfth birthday. Brona was an excellent baker and she had made a round red velvet cake with cream cheese frosting. On top was a candle in the shape of the number twelve.

Their parents had been fighting since they got home from church and the whole family was on edge that day. Kevin leaned against the stove with his arms crossed in irritation and everyone just wanted the *celebration* to be over. Laura was anxious about being the center of attention on a good day, let alone when everyone was angry and she knew the slightest thing would set her parents off, so she wasted no time leaning over the cake to make her wish.

Kevin let out a noisy sigh. "Can we get on with it?"

Laura squeezed her eyes shut and wished for the kitchen to explode, taking them all straight to God. Their youth leader spent most of his time scaring them to death with lessons about what happens in Hell to young girls who have wicked thoughts. He claimed he was trying to save them from lustful encounters with sex and drugs, but she wondered if the torturous punishment applied to all wicked thoughts. Would she get the opportunity to explain herself before being sent to Hell for her wish or would she just wake up bobbing around in a lake of fire?

Regardless, it seemed that something up there was, at least half-heartedly, paying attention to her. There was no explosion, but when she blew out the candle, a thin stream of flame moved across the cake and on to a pile of paper napkins. She slapped at the napkins and the little flame jumped in the palm of her hand. She clapped her hands together and a tiny puff of smoke escaped through the gap between her thumbs. She and Sarah exchanged a wide-eyed glance while Brona glowered at them from across the room.

Kevin hadn't noticed the incident but later that night Brona shoved Laura against the bunk bed ladder, demanding information. "What did you do to that candle?"

"I don't know, nothing."

"I'm watching you, girl. You've got the devil in you."

In spite of Brona's freak out, or perhaps because of it, they enjoyed their growing secret. They could do things and see things that others couldn't, but it had never been scary before Sarah encountered the screaming thing in the mirror.

In the library, they settled on an encyclopedia of sorts. It was called "A Modern Guide to Spirits, Ghosts and Fairies."

"Ugh. There are no pictures, so you won't recognize it," Laura complained. Even so, they sat shoulder to shoulder at the table, reading every single entry.

"Aren't you ladies supposed to be in school?" A short, kindly looking woman wearing a brown corduroy wrap around skirt over a cream-colored body suit peered at them from behind enormous round eyeglasses. She leaned on the desk and crossed her ankles.

Laura liked her tall boots but was afraid to tell her. She'd wanted some like that, the kind with zippers, for a while. Everyone wore cowboy boots in Chuparosa, including Laura, but she thought the zippers and high heels were more fun and grown up. Brona said she couldn't have a pair because they would make her look like a whore, but Laura didn't think Rhonda looked like a whore.

They knew the librarian from church but hadn't seen her in several Sundays. Rhonda Deschene had recently lost her husband, Ed, so the girls assumed that crisis warranted some sort of religious free pass for mourning purposes. They noted that she seemed cheerful enough though.

They'd once overheard Brona gossiping about how Ed was a rat bastard who had beaten Rhonda senseless on several occasions. He also happened to be a diabetic with a literal bloodlust for sweets. Word in the

Wednesday Ladies Worship was that she fed him her blue-ribbon desserts until he died. There was talk of a substantial insurance policy and the nosy ladies were all agog, wondering if Rhonda would skip town with the money.

As far as Laura and Sarah were concerned, Rhonda was their new hero and Ed Deschene could rot with his cinnamon rolls.

Sarah looked down at her lap. "We were doing some research."

"On ghosts? On a Tuesday morning?" Rhonda pressed.

Laura slouched in her chair. "On screaming things, actually."

"What, like banshees?" Both girls sat up straight and blinked at her.

She laughed, "You've never heard the term, 'screaming like a banshee'?"

They had not. Rhonda chuckled again. "Geez, when I was your age, all I researched was boys." She shook her head, but before she walked away, added, "I'll be at the desk if you need my help."

They looked at each other and turned to the B's and sure enough:

*Banshee: A supernatural being in Irish and other Celtic folklore whose mournful wailing, screaming or lamentation was believed to foretell the death of a member of the family of the person who heard the spirit.*

Brona was outside talking to a police officer when the girls returned home. He reported to them, with his condolences, that Kevin had been killed in a construction accident.

It made the girls uncomfortable when Brona's friends tried to comfort them because, after he died, they couldn't call what they were feeling grief. Later in life, they did feel robbed of the opportunity to learn Kevin's side of the story, but it was impossible to mourn someone they didn't really know. At best, he'd merely tolerated their presence. His hateful relationship with their mother fueled their confusion about him and they would forever associate his memory with fear and mystery.

On the rare occasion when Brona showed any related emotion it seemed to them that, more than anything, he was a dream of hers that had died. She may have been telling herself as much as the girls, but on the day of his funeral, she insisted they'd better "just deal with it." So, they did.

Their main takeaway from the whole ordeal was that their secret was no longer a game and that their lives would be spent not just managing themselves around their mother, but around everyone they would ever meet.

## Chapter Two

Sarah parked her Jeep Cherokee in the five-story garage, and they made their way through the maze of unadorned, latte-colored buildings that comprised the Sun City Partners Medical Group. The directory in the courtyard pointed them to a small structure tucked away in the very back of the facility.

A blue and yellow striped awning over a set of automatic doors was illuminated by wrought iron coach lights on either side of it. A small metal plaque fastened under one of the lights welcomed them to New Peace Hospice.

"It smells awful in here," Audi complained.

"Let's find your Auntie."

"Do we sign in?" Audi looked around but found nothing like a reception desk.

"It's designed to look like a house, honey. The dying and their families are more comfortable if it feels like home."

Audi curled her lip. "Okay sure, if you live in Hell House."

The entryway led to a sitting area made up of four love seats arranged in a square. End tables next to each one were strewn with magazines. Along the wall behind them was a refrigerator and a counter with a single cup coffee machine, an electric kettle, and a tiny sink. Styrofoam cups, tea bags and coffee pods were arranged neatly on a shelf next to the sink.

On the far end of the counter was a clear plastic container that held business cards for local mortuaries and estate planners. Lining the walls were doors leading to the patient rooms, and outside each room was a piece of construction paper taped to the wall with the occupant's name handwritten in block script.

They found Laura seated on one of the loveseats reading from her Kindle. Audi plopped down beside her and swiped the device from her hands. "Sylvia Plath, Auntie? How dramatic."

Sarah sat on the arm of the seat. "What have you heard?"

"They gave her quite a cocktail so she's in and out of consciousness, but you can go in and see her."

The older women hesitated at the door labeled, "Brona Deane", while Audi approached the bed whispering, "Hi NaNa.".

"Go on," Laura prodded. "I've been here all morning."

Sarah shuffled in slowly and sat on the end of the bed. "Hey, Mom."

Brona's labored breathing made speaking difficult so she lay there silently, eyes darting from her youngest daughter to her oldest, and then to her grandchild. Sarah thought she noticed something new in her mother's eyes. Was it fear? What Sarah couldn't know was that in the hospital, the night before, Brona had heard the witch's death knock. And yes, she was very much afraid.

When Laura left the day before, Brona shooed away the long-suffering Nurse's Assistant who came to take her vitals. She lay dozing lightly, waiting for the latest dose of morphine to overtake her senses when the first knock came so loudly that she jerked in her bed and let out a bewildered yelp. Assuming an orderly slammed a cart of some kind into the door, she pressed the call button.

"Yes, ma'am?"

"Can you tell those idiots to be more careful?"

"Which idiots, Mrs. Deane?" The charge nurse was low on patience and made a mental note to increase Brona's morphine drip.

"Whatever they're moving out there is slamming against my door."

"I don't think there's anyone out there, but I'll take care of it."

Brona flopped back on to her pillow in frustration. "God, Laura," she griped to the emptiness, "this place you put me in is a dump."

The second knock came just after midnight. Even louder than the first, Brona's bed shook from the force of it and a new pressure in her chest pinned her to the mattress. After fumbling the call panel through the side rail, she made a frantic visual search, but there was no one to yell for in the private room Laura had secured for her. She lay motionless for the next few hours with only the sounds of the IV drip and her uneven breathing to complement the darkness.

At 3am, her bed began to shake again. The needle tugged at the tape on her arm as the IV stand wobbled behind her and toppled to the floor. With her lips trembling and her mind racing, Brona pressed on her arm to keep the tube in place, though she knew the fluids were no longer doing her any good. Three knocks meant her death was certain, but how would it come? Would it be right then?

She was gasping for breath, tears seeped from the corners of her eyes, and she felt she might suffocate from fear. Grabbing the bedrail, she marshaled all of her strength to sit up, but the rail hadn't been properly secured so she lost her balance and slipped off the side of the bed, smacking hard against the tile.

On the other side of the door, the Nurse's Assistant took several deep breaths and told herself that it would only take a couple of minutes and that she wouldn't take anything Mrs. Deane said personally. Bitch or not, the woman *was* dying, and probably pretty pissed off about it. She squared her shoulders and opened the door.

The third and final knock then slammed against the window, exploding shards of glass across the room. The Nurse's Assistant screamed and threw herself on top of Brona, covering the older woman with her body and shielding her own head with her hands.

Surrounded later by her family in the safety of the Hospice room, Brona had never felt more alone, and she physically shuddered.

Sarah took her hand. "Mom? What are you thinking about?"

Brona turned her head away and Sarah's shoulders sagged. She'd threatened to kill herself a hundred times, but it would seem that Brona Deane was actually terrified of dying.

Audi ran her hand over the quilt on the bed. "Look NaNa, daisies-your favorite."


The next morning Laura and Sarah met early on one of the many hiking paths that snaked through the mountains. A handful were maintained by the county, but most trails were made by the locals. Many of whom, Sarah included, could walk out their back doors straight into the desert wilderness.

They hadn't been able to connect with one another since Brona's illness worsened and since the Ford Canyon trail joined the Mesquite Trail right behind Sarah's property, it was the most convenient place. In what amounted to just under four miles of moderate hiking, the sisters could catch up and get some exercise.

The animals were enjoying the spring weather that day as much as the humans. A family of quail crossed their path with no less than ten babies in tow. Springtime in the Sonoran Desert also meant the cacti were in bloom and Ford Canyon trail was home to a forest of Teddy Bear Cholla that had recently sprouted hundreds of yellow and white flowers.

The women knew Teddy Bear Cholla by its local name, jumping cactus. It was infamous for seemingly *jumping* at passersby who got too close. Arizonans knew to steer clear, but tourists often found themselves covered in tiny, painful spines. The spines were so short and so numerous that they looked soft, and the cactus had a stout body with small arms, like a teddy bear. Sarah had been convinced at an early age that the plants were used as traps by the Other Side, a place full of beings she referred to as desert fairies, to keep humans from getting too close.

They were alone on the trail with only the crunch, crunch, crunch of their hiking boots in the dirt and the breeze in the bushes. They both loved the desert and the peaceful refuge it had always provided them, even in their darkest times. *Especially in their darkest times.* After a mile or so, Laura broke the silence.

"It was nice of Audi to mom-sit today."

"Well, Mom might not be happy about it. That girl doesn't put up with anything." Sarah shook her head. "Did she tell you that her biology teacher got a little too interested in her progress last week? He offered to meet her for 'coffee', so she sent a direct message to his wife on Instagram. Nothing fazes that girl."

"I'm sure she gets fazed, she just doesn't tell her mom about it," Laura laughed, "Brian only tells me what he thinks I can handle."

Sarah wrinkled her brow. "Yeah. I'm just happy she's found her path. Rueben made fun when she decided on nursing, you know, because of her grades in high school. So far, she's happy with her choice."

Laura's heart sank a little. "At least she's still at home." She had been bursting with pride when Northern Arizona University recruited her son, Brian, to their swim team but was thoroughly broken hearted when he left home.

They took a slight detour off the county trail and started down the wash running through a shallow part of the canyon, stopping short when something darted across their path.

Sarah grabbed at her sister's arm. "Look at that!" A petite kit fox stood not fifty feet away, eyeing them suspiciously.

"Is that a fox?" Laura reached for her phone to take a picture, but it scurried away to the bushes before she could get a shot. "Damn, I missed it."

"That's a guard and we're too close to something." Sarah gestured toward a deep crevice in the canyon wall.

"Sarah, sometimes a fox is just a fox."

"Maybe."

Once Sarah learned the banshees could contact her, she became obsessed with finding more fairies. She dreamed of having a group of kind little friends, like in the children's stories. Rhonda lectured them often about dangerous fairies and gave them book after book backing up her words of warning.

Even so, Sarah was convinced that the beings on the Other Side were some sort of desert Fae and just knew that if only she could figure out how to properly communicate with them, they would welcome her friendship. There had been plenty of opportunities, but her efforts thus far had been in vain.

As a teenager, a strange jackrabbit caught her attention one afternoon when they were partying in the desert with some friends. It would not have been unusual but for its size. It was as tall as a toddler with ears at least a foot long, and weirder still, it didn't run away from them. They were drinking and loud and the boys were racing around on motor bikes, stirring up dirt and rocks. Still, the rabbit sat motionless.

She looked around. *Did no one else see it?* The rabbit sat still, watching her. As she took a step toward it, her vision blurred, and her head felt fuzzy as if she were tipsy. Finally, it slowly hopped away, pausing to look back every few feet like it expected her to follow. It led her about a half mile from her friends before darting into a thicket of Cholla cactus covered with orange and red blooms.

The smell of lemon and vanilla was like candy to her senses and she was entranced. Bending to pick a flower, she noticed the rabbit crouching at the base of the plant. For the first time, she saw that its eyes took up nearly half of its face, and when they blinked at her, she swooned and fell to her knees.

It reached up, picked a blossom from the cactus, and held it out. She was so moved by the gesture that she leaned over to inhale the scent, but when she was close enough, the creature shoved the blossom in her face. The flower was large and covered both her mouth and nose and when she discovered she couldn't breathe, the rabbit grinned wide, revealing a mouth full of sharp teeth. Sarah struggled to turn away, but it was much stronger than her, holding the back of her head and pushing on the flower until she fell backward for lack of air and passed out.

Laura found her lying on the ground, unconscious and surrounded by flower petals and it was three weeks before Sarah recovered her sense of smell. That sneaky rabbit had lured her into a trap and Sarah's heart was broken.

Rhonda tried to comfort her. "They might not be fairies, Sarah. We don't know what's on the Other Side. We don't know what they are."

"I know what they are." Sarah had sobbed, "I just don't know why they hate me."

Sarah never gave up on her quest but as the girls grew older, the more wary of the Other Side they became.

Laura pointed to the trail above them. "Alright, I don't want any trouble today, let's climb back up."

If they annoyed something, it might only drop a rock on their heads as a warning, but it could just as easily send a bobcat their way, so it was better not to push their luck. They climbed out of the canyon and, once safely on the designated trail, Sarah changed the subject.

"How are things going with Sheriff Sexy?"

Laura's eyes reddened, but she fought back the tears. "They're not. He's no longer interested in dark, dangerous, messy women, like me."

Sarah stopped and faced her. "He said that to you? What a dick. Damn, I had high hopes for him. Rueben really liked him, too."

Laura laughed. "Rueben is still allowed to like him. Don't they work in the same building?"

Sarah sniffed. "No, he's not." She knew that Rueben Soto would never be told who he could be friends with, especially not by his wife, but it felt good to say it. She would never admit it, but she liked Sebastian, too, and had hoped her sister's relationship with him would work out.

Further, she would never admit that her disappointment for Laura was a bit selfish. She'd thought if her sister could find love in middle age, then maybe life wasn't so bad outside of the relative safety of a marriage. That moron had broken her heart, but Laura could live alone and be happy if she had to. She'd done it for years before Sebastian Scott showed up. It was one of her big sister's superpowers.

Sarah had never lived alone though, and the ever-numbing unpleasantness of grasping at the frayed edges of her marriage seemed preferable to the raw misery Laura was trying so hard to cover up.

Laura waved off Sarah's concern. "It's okay. I'm getting a dog. You know, we've never had familiars and that's probably bad luck." She thought wistfully of her son's childhood, "I should have given Brian a dog."

"Brian is just fine, and I can't get one. Rueben is allergic to dogs, and he hates cats."

Laura picked up a small stick and waved it in the air. "You need to make him rethink that."

"I don't cast spells on my husband."

"I know. He's very lucky and you need a dog." She tossed the stick away and changed the subject again. "Did you get your first retirement check?"

Sarah grinned. "I did!"

"Teaching fifth graders for twenty years." Laura shuddered. "How did you not lose your mind?"

"I kind of miss them, and you didn't warn me about the post-retirement existential crisis."

Laura shrugged. "Is it really a crisis? We worked for the state for twenty years, our kids are grown, I'm getting my business off the ground, you and Rueben can travel, and we're not even fifty yet.

She spread her arms wide and spun her body in a circle. "We have all this freedom and it's a whole new chapter of life."

"When all this business with Mom is over," Sarah said. "Can you imagine? It being over? I mean?"

Laura put a hand to her forehead. "Just stop. I don't know how to feel about that."

"Alright, speaking of business…"

Laura's face brightened. "I have a lot of late nights, but I'm keeping up. I've got a big order for the Wishing Tree in Flagstaff, so I'll run it up there in a couple of days, and visit Brian, too. I've got to get the Jeep serviced before I leave though."

"It's not giving you any trouble."

Laura shrugged. "I know, but still."

After high school graduation, Laura had worked as a bank teller in Phoenix. Her boyfriend at the time gave her a ride to work every day but she was saving money to buy her own car. There was a Ford Mustang she'd been eyeing in the local paper, but the guy wanted three thousand dollars for it. Since she only had twenty-six hundred, she lost out, but in the late eighties, old Mustangs were everywhere.

Brona showed up at the bank one day, very excited. "I've found a car for you. It seems very reliable and it's only two thousand dollars."

Laura was suspicious, but desperately wanted to believe her mother would do that for her.

"Just give me the money and I'll take care of everything."

Ignoring a sizable sense of dread, Laura withdrew the money and handed it over. Of course, there was no car, and she never did find out what Brona used the money for.

"That was most of my savings!" she had sobbed.

Brona was unrepentant. "You are so selfish. I knew you wouldn't have given it to me if I'd asked, so what was I supposed to do, Sherlock?"

Laura took what remained of her money and purchased a bank repossession that overheated constantly, leaving her stranded at nearly every Phoenix intersection that summer.

Not even Arley, the mechanical wizard who owned Chuparosa Gas and Service, could help her.

"I can only do so much, Laura," he'd said sympathetically, "that thing is on its last legs."

With Rhonda's connections, she landed an administrative state job and left home that fall. Right before Christmas, the car died three miles from her little apartment so she unscrewed the license plate and left it on the side of the road. From then on, she only bought new vehicles and had them serviced religiously.

## Chapter Three

Mesquite Trail picked up where Ford Canyon folded into the mountains and when they came around the ridge, the women froze as they spotted an enormous German Shepherd trotting straight toward them. It wore no collar, and they could see no owner nearby. It was the biggest dog they'd ever seen, the kind that could tear them to shreds.

"Shit," Sarah said, "what do we do?"

The dog stopped in front of Laura and gave her knee a nudge with his nose before sitting at her feet.

"Hey, buddy." She smiled nervously and dug a peanut butter energy ball out of a pouch on her hip. He wagged his tail, so she cautiously held it out to him. "Do you want a snack?" He sniffed at it for a second, then gobbled it up.

Laura took a knee and scratched him on the head. "Do you have a name, big guy?" The dog licked her hand and then her face.

Sarah put her hands on her hips and looked around. "Where did he come from?"

Someone they hadn't seen before let out a whistle and the dog backed away. It was then that they noticed a man about a hundred yards down the trail. From what they could tell, he was a typical hiker wearing khaki pants, a black long-sleeved t-shirt and boots. His hair was dark and wavy, and fell long across his shoulders. He was too far for them to gather more information, but he was playing a dangerous game with his fellow hikers.

"Hey!" Laura yelled at him. "Your dog needs a leash!"

He whistled again and the dog whimpered, backing farther away. When the man whistled a third time, the dog let out a low growl, turned, and dashed to its owner.

Sarah raised an eyebrow at her sister. "You were saying? About getting a dog?"

"Okay, fine. So, time to go?"

"Yup."

As they reached the trailhead, Sarah's phone rang.

Audi's voice was somber. "You should come."

When they arrived at the Hospice, Audi was stretching her legs by the kitchenette.

"I'm waiting for the nurse to leave," she said. "They drugged NaNa up again, so she's been sleeping hard. On second thought, we should get an update before the shift change."

Laura went with her while Sarah made herself some coffee, putting off the inevitable.

Laura and Audi stood at the doorway of Brona's room. Her mother's body was eerily still except for the slow rise and fall of her chest. A tall, gaunt woman stood over Brona's bed with her back to them and she wasn't just thin, Laura noted. She was skeletal.

"Are her actual bones sticking out?" Audi whispered.

The nurse's long hair was gathered in a low ponytail at the nape of her neck. Laura thought it must have been the shadowy lighting, but her hair had an iridescent shine to it that seemed to reflect throughout the room.

The other hospice nurses they'd met wore navy blue scrubs, but this one was dressed in powder blue. There was no stethoscope around her neck, and no watch on her wrist. She carried no phone, and nothing bulged from her pockets.

Laura had spent the last month practically living in the hospital with her mother and she'd never seen a nurse who wasn't loaded down with everything from rolls of tape and scissors to needles and markers.

A light breeze fluttered at the curtains on the other side of the room, but Brona's window wasn't open.

Laura reached across her niece's body. "Audi, get back."

The nurse whirled around and grinned at them with long sharp teeth. Her eyes glowed red in the dimness.

"Okay so she's not a real nurse." Audi backed away, but her feet felt as if they were moving through quick sand.

Laura's vision blurred and she felt the floor shift under her feet. The nurse shoved her way between them and charged into the waiting room.

Audi grabbed the door jamb for balance and muttered, "Bitch."

Dazed, they stared as the nurse took Sarah by the shoulders. The paper cup fell from her hands, hitting the thick carpet with a thud and splashing coffee all over their feet. The skin on the banshee's face sank inward until only its bare skull remained. Sarah closed her eyes and tried to turn her head away, but the banshee shook her violently. It brought itself nose to nose with her...and screamed.

"Fucking fairies." Laura regained her balance and started toward her sister. The banshee hissed at her with annoyance but released Sarah and vanished through the corner of the room.


At 12:15 a.m. Brona watched as one by one, six crows landed on the ledge outside the window. The low bookcase on the inside, directly under the window, housed titles like "Dying Well," "Living at the End of Life," and "Being Mortal." Her daughters were asleep in the high-backed chairs on either side of the bookcase and Audi sat cross-legged on the floor, playing with her phone.

She studied them, her abominations. She supposed she could call out and bring them to her. She could wake them and possibly have time to tell them all about the horrible mistakes she'd made. She could tell them all the things she should have told them from the beginning, all the things they didn't realize that they desperately needed to know. Instead, she simply closed her eyes, and without any commotion at all, Brona Deane passed away.

## *Chapter Four*

Laura threw her backpack on the kitchen table, selected
an orange from a bowl on the counter and sank down
on a chair. March was the perfect time for being outside
in Arizona and she'd been on the trails since before
dawn. The snowbirds were never out that early in the
day, so she'd had a very peaceful morning.

When he was little, she used to prop Brian in a sling
on her back and take him out to watch the sun rise. It
was the closest thing to a religious experience she'd ever
had. When he could walk, it was all she could do to keep
up with him on their morning outings. He ran after
lizards and rabbits, and she taught him to watch for
rattlesnakes and scorpions. As a teenager, he lost
interest in rising early, but on the rare occasions she
could get him to go, they talked and talked. She smiled
to herself as the memories flooded her mind.

He was getting a ride down from school and she
couldn't wait to see him. It would be the only highlight
on the day's agenda as Brona's funeral was at noon.

Since Sarah's house was much larger, it made sense for her to host. Laura had offered to help pay, but Rueben wouldn't allow it. What he didn't realize was that his sister-in-law was so grateful not to have those people in her house that she would have gone into debt to pay for the entire funeral.

Brona was the closest thing to a Saint that the local Baptists could get. Laura stared dumbfounded once when Brona's preacher told her the Wednesday Women's Ministry had suffered a gaping hole in leadership since Brona illness. One of the many things he didn't know was that when he asked Brona, years earlier, to take over Wednesday nights, she'd nearly killed her husband that day.

Kevin and Brona frequently had their most vicious fights on Sunday mornings. That week, she slammed the backdoor so hard that the window shattered. When Kevin swung at her, she swung back, barely missing his jugular vein with a shard of glass.

After that, Brona made Laura sit in the front seat with her dad on the way home from church and her parents didn't speak for a week. The backdoor had cardboard and duct tape in the window space until they moved out.

Unable to avoid the inevitable funeral any longer, Laura went to her bathroom, turned on the shower and got undressed. While waiting for the water to heat, she stared in the mirror and gasped. She had been noticing more and more that it was Brona's face in her reflection.

She told herself, "You're not her," and turned away, but Laura didn't notice that Brona's reflection remained in the mirror as she stepped into the shower.

Sarah piled the platters of mini chimichangas, taquitos, and quesadillas that they'd ordered from Marco's Restaurant atop her kitchen counter while Audi arranged bags of chips and salsa.

"Are we feeding the whole town?" Rueben poked his head into a bag of chips and grabbed a handful.

"Maybe, Rueben. She did have a lot of friends."

"So, you better get ready, huh Dad?" Audi poked him in the belly. "All the Pastors will be here today."

Rueben threw his head back in frustration. "Aw, Jesus."

"He's not coming, as far as I know." Audi grinned and shooed him away.

Rueben wasn't really angry with his wife. Brona was her mother, after all. Damn if that old woman didn't hate him though. Brona had called him a loser to his face more than once. He was the Director of Facilities at the Chuparosa Government building that housed the Sheriff's office, Justice Court and the utility company. But when he met Sarah, he was a young man mopping those floors himself and Brona could never contain her disgust for him.

Picking a fight on the day of her mother's funeral ranked high in the 'horrible husband behavior' category, so he did as he was told, and even wore a new shirt.

Laura and Brian arrived early to help set up, but there wasn't much to do. The food was out and the family was watching television, grimly waiting on the guests.

Audi jumped up to greet them. "Brian!"

The cousins were close, and he was happy to see her. Audi was a year younger, but not behind him in college since she'd taken advantage of the community college options offered when she was a junior in high school.

She'd been able to get a head start on her introductory college classes by taking them along with her regular classes. Though she wasn't the best student, her grades were good enough to get her into the program and when she graduated high school, a coveted spot in nursing school waited for her.

Brian went the athletic route. Tall and broad shouldered, he was a natural at the butterfly stroke and Northern Arizona University had noticed. So, he agreed to trade roughly six hours a day in their pool for an electrical engineering degree.

Laura swore that Brian didn't inherit any of the Deane powers, but Brona always regarded him suspiciously, and kept him at arm's length. His mother never tried to influence his opinion, but he couldn't forgive Brona's treatment of her. He wasn't grieving the death of his grandmother, and that felt very strange.

The doorbell rang and Laura straightened her dress. "Okay, let's do this."

Pastor Clarke was the first to arrive. In life, Brona attended the local Baptist Church, but Sarah was a member of the New Sanctuary, and Andrew Clarke was their leader. He was an electrician, and that paid his bills, but his true occupation was God's work. Or, what he believed to be God's work. The New Sanctuary might as well have been called *the home for mixed up adults who were traumatized and damaged by their hypocritical, evangelical families*. In a town like Chuparosa, that home was nearly bursting at the seams.

"Pastor Clarke!" Laura exclaimed, ushering him in.

His smile was warm as he scolded her. "I've told you a hundred times to call me Drew. I fixed a switch in your bedroom this week, for God's sake."

She lowered her eyelids in spite of herself. He was in his early fifties, six-foot something, with ash blonde hair and the deepest blue eyes. He had a small bandage taped across one knuckle and the callouses on his palms brushed roughly against her skin as he took her hand in both of his.

Andrew's hands told the story of a man who liked to work on things, and she was intrigued by him. Laura avoided church and kept him at a friendly distance but, if pressed, she would have to admit to being more than a little bit curious about his views on pre-marital...everything.

Unlike the Baptists, he knew Brona the way her daughters did. She couldn't stand him and what she called his "blasphemous teachings." The sisters, however, were grateful for his constant presence and support. Laura led Drew to the living room where he shook Rueben's hand and nodded to the younger adults.

Audi leaned against Brian and whispered, "He's like, old man hot."

"He's like, thirty years older than you, so maybe you should steer clear of the felonies."

"I'm over eighteen, so there's no felony."

He made a gagging noise. "Shut up."

The doorbell rang again, and this time Brian answered.

"Brian, look at you!" Rhonda handed him a scrumptious smelling hot dish.

He took it to the stove and tore off the foil, revealing tater tot casserole, a Chuparosa funeral favorite. He and Audi grabbed forks and there was no way that the pan would make it to the guest tables.

"Ladies!"

Laura and Sarah rushed to hug her. Rhonda genuinely adored the Deane sisters. With no children of her own and no husband, she gave them much of her time and energy. In return, they doted on her like a cherished matriarch.

Her personal experience with witchcraft was limited to what the universe was willing to help her manifest on her own. With the right ingredients and a focused intention, she could be quite formidable in her own right, but the Deanes exhibited power like she'd never seen.

Having been a librarian in the pre-internet eighties, her access to knowledge was unmatched in Chuparosa. So, she exposed them to every magical, historical, and scientific source she could find. Once, when a sixteen-year-old Laura burned down the shed in her backyard, Rhonda was there with a lesson on backdraft. The poor girl had assumed that opening a window would let the smoke out but almost blew up the whole property.

Beyond that, they frequently had questions they didn't dare take to their mother, lest they be punished for a new sin of some sort. Laura and Sarah were gifted and good-hearted, more or less, so Rhonda was mystified by Brona's decision to shame and condemn them. One could argue she was simply ignorant and afraid, but Rhonda didn't believe that for a minute. They lived in Chuparosa, after all.

"Ooh, baby tacos," she cooed. "Are these from Marco's? Did you know Blanca is pregnant?"

Laura scooped a chip through the salsa. "I did not. I'll take her some ginger pops tomorrow."

"Thanks for being here, Rhonda," Sarah whispered.

"Are you kidding, I wouldn't miss the who's who of hypocrisy today for anything."

Over the next two hours, a steady stream of Brona's friends came and went, and everyone had a great story about her. Laura cried when they described her mother as selfless, charitable, kind, and devoted because they weren't wrong. Brona was all of those things, she just didn't share that side of herself with her daughters.

Rueben found her on a chaise outside and handed her a fresh glass of wine. "You okay, sister?"

"Not today." She pointed to a group from the Women's Ministry reminiscing about the work Brona had done on the food boxes at Christmastime.

"Rueben, we didn't know that person. We knew a—"

Rueben whispered low, "A bitch."

She giggled though her tears. "They loved her though."

He grunted, "Her kids were the best part of her."

When Sarah and Drew joined them, Rueben locked eyes with the preacher, nodding at Laura. Drew didn't know Laura as well as he knew her sister, but he did know that she was the one who wore her heart on her sleeve. She mourned the loss of a mother she never had, and his heart swelled with sympathy. His own mother had been, at best, an impersonal authority in his life. At worst, a sovereign capable of vicious degradation.

Sarah, always more stoic, stroked Laura's hair. "They just knew a different side of her is all."

Drew tried to lighten the mood a little. "Laura, is Sebastian working today?"

Rueben leapt up and swiped his hand across his throat in the 'cut it out' signal, but it was too late.

Laura's eye twitched slightly. "I have no idea."

"Oh, I thought," Drew stammered, "I thought you two were…"

She let him off the hook with a wave of her hand. "That's okay, so did I."

He winced. *Oh, great. Way to step in it.* "I'm sorry, Laura. I'm not always an insensitive ass. It's all kindness and class from here on out today, I promise."

Laura stood up and put a reassuring hand on his shoulder. "*You* are not the ass, Drew."

She left them and went inside to the guest bathroom, cursing Sebastian under her breath as a newly familiar tingle washed over her skin and a flush crept into her cheeks. *Good God, a hot flash? Is that what we're doing today?* She steadied herself against the doorframe as the heatwave rushed across her chest and over the back of her neck.

Late in her forties, perimenopause had shown up and gifted her with erratic temperature control and a heightened sex drive. Living single in the country's hottest state was getting more uncomfortable by the day, which did not bode well for someone doing her best to age gracefully. She suddenly empathized with every cranky old lady she'd ever met. They weren't mean, they were just hot, in every sense of the word.

In the mirror, she took note of the shower curtain behind her and smiled at the seashells and starfish.

Though she'd never seen it, Sarah's obsession with the ocean showed up in every piece of the bathroom's decor. Hair soaked and makeup trashed, Laura took a washcloth from a driftwood shelf next to the sink and turned on the cold-water faucet.

She peered at her reflection again, vexed that her mother's face returned her gaze. Shaking out her hair, she jumped back in alarm when only part of her image moved, leaving a pale profile next to hers in the mirror. She whirled around but no one was there.

The hair on her arms rose in warning. *Please, no.* She returned to the sink and put the washcloth back under the faucet, but the water streamed so hot that it burned her skin. She jerked her red hands away and held them to her chest. Something rustled from behind but she took her time while shutting off the faucet, hanging the washcloth, and turning around. Fresh beads of sweat formed across her forehead and her heart raced, but she forced herself to take a step toward the tub. She stretched out her arm and took another step, pausing as her hand grazed the fabric of the shower curtain.

Her breath had been coming in short gasps, so she forced herself to inhale deeply, hold it, and let it out slowly. Somewhat calmed, she closed her hand around the fabric and threw open the curtain, then clapped her hand to her mouth to stifle a scream and staggered backward against the sink.

Brona was sitting in the tub with her knees held to her chest. "So, drove another man away, did you?" Her mother sneered.

The breathing exercise abandoned; Laura succumbed to full on hyperventilation while trying to process the vision in front of her. *She must be a ghost. She's just a ghost. Of course, she would be a ghost.*

"Mom? Mom, is that you?"

The water came on in the sink behind her and in the shower and steam began to fill the room.

"What do think you're doing, Sherlock?"

Laura grabbed a mermaid soap dish from the sink and hurled it at the tub, but Brona dodged and let it crash against the tile. Then she picked it up, stepped on to the bathmat and held it out. In shock, Laura let it fall between them, then Brona gave her a chilling smile, opened the bathroom door, and ran down the hall.

Laura ran after her to the main bedroom, which had a glass patio door that had been left open, through which she followed Brona outside. The guests went quiet as she burst through, turning in circles and gasping for breath.

"Uh, Mom?" Brian and Audi took her by the arms.

"I'm fine," she stammered. "I just...did you see something run out here? Out the bedroom door?"

Brian and Audi exchanged glances. "No, Mom, just you."


He wasn't sure what to say about it, and it was none of his business, but Drew had followed Laura in the house, feeling awful after bringing up Sebastian's name. Based on their few interactions he imagined her to be a handful, but Bash seemed sturdy enough and more than willing to take on the challenge. Maybe he was wrong about the lawman, but he would never dare to call himself an authority on romantic relationships.

Laura was conflicted about her mother and that's where Drew was confident that he could be of assistance if he could get her to open up to him.

He'd stopped short when he saw the bathroom door close and decided to pay her a call later in the week; but had just turned on his heel when a clatter and a muffled shriek echoed from in the room. The door burst open, and something jumped out, scowling in his direction. At first, he thought it was an animal of some kind, but while small, it was human in stature, with long, sinewy limbs and black eyes. It skittered away from him and down the hall to one of the bedrooms with Laura chasing it out to the backyard, where it disappeared from the porch.

Laura found Sarah in the kitchen, clearly tired of the day's events and filling up a water bottle with equal parts vodka and cranberry juice.

"Sarah, I saw her."

"Who?"

"Mom."

"What?"

"In the bathroom."

Sarah gaped at her and poured her drink down the drain.

"I'm serious, I just saw her."

Rueben poked his head into the kitchen. "The preacher and Rhonda are leaving."

Sarah clung to the older woman a little longer than she intended when they said goodbye.

"You okay, sweetie?"

"Yeah, it's just been a long day."

Drew spoke low in Laura's ear when she led them to the door. "Listen I know this is not a good time, but I need to talk to you about something when you get the chance. Please, call me when it's convenient."

She liked Drew very much, but it would never be convenient for her to call him. She did not share her sister's need to grapple with the mysteries of God and the universe.

Rueben had begun to pace like a caged animal, so Laura and Brian left right behind them, bringing Audi along to hang out with her cousin for the evening.

Laura gripped her sister's hand and said, "Call me later."

Sarah closed the door after them and turned to face her husband who, now that the house had emptied, was done behaving himself.

"Good thing we spent all this money to be miserable for a day." He grabbed a beer and went into their bedroom, closing the door behind him.

Sarah flopped down on the couch and leaned back with her eyes closed. She was not sad, but a few tears found their way down her cheeks as an overwhelming sense of relief made its way through her body. *It's finally over.*

Rummaging around in the entertainment center, she found the remote control and cued up Netflix. If ever there was a night she deserved to zone out in front of her favorite show, that was the time. She whispered, "fuck it" to herself and went to the kitchen for another glass of wine.

As she returned to the living room, the glass slipped from her hand and shattered on the floor. Her mother sat where she had been, legs crossed at the ankles in her favorite prim, judgmental pose.

"Hmph," Brona nodded in the direction of Sarah's bedroom, "I told you. You married your father."

*No, no, no.* Sarah squeezed her eyes closed. Brona's ghost was gone when she opened them and without a second thought, she pressed number one in her cell phone contacts.

When Laura answered, Sarah said, "What the hell did I just see?"

## Chapter Five

Laura spread cream cheese on a bagel, took a bite, frowned, and put it down. Restless and anxious, she leaned against the counter and rubbed her temples. She'd still been awake, musing over her mother's unsettling reappearance, when Brian came home just after midnight. She needed to focus because Sarah and Audi were coming over so, anxious or not, she popped a pod into her new Nespresso machine and pressed the button.

She'd ordered the appliance in a late night, wine-induced Amazon shopping spree after Bash broke them up. It was a pleasant surprise when it turned out to be her new favorite way to have coffee. She frowned again. *Stupid Bash.*

Brona had only met him a couple of times but liked him very much. *That should have been the first red flag.* She was certain Laura would screw up the relationship, and even mentioned that to him once. Laura scrunched up her nose. *You were right, Mom-are you happy?*

She tossed the bagel in the trash, put the plate in the sink and stared out the window, sipping her coffee. On the sill was a potted violet, a large amethyst crystal, and a tiny tin man.

Her mother loved the Wizard of Oz and collected miniature figurines of the characters. When it became clear that Brona would be in the hospital long-term, Laura went to her apartment to clean out the refrigerator and gather the mail. She took the tin man and placed it on Brona's hospital nightstand.

She either never noticed, or thought it was a stupid idea because she never said anything to Laura about it. So, when Brona moved to the hospice facility, the little tin man moved to Laura's windowsill. She gave it a flick with her fingers, toppling it over.

She took a peek in Brian's room. He would be asleep for half the day, so she closed his door and returned to the kitchen. She gave her plate a rinse and opened the dishwasher but the plate slipped from her fingers with a crash when she saw the tiny tin man standing upright on the windowsill.

Her hands shook a little as she carried a glass spray bottle and some scissors to the courtyard on her back porch. The small, pergola covered space was her favorite feature of the little Spanish colonial house. She conducted her spell work and meditation out there and, in the cooler months, used the space for exercise and entertaining as well.

The floor, like most of the outdoor spaces around the house, was paved in terra cotta tiles. The iron rods that made up the pergola were loosely covered in creeping fig vines which let in just enough sun to keep her plants happy and kept it shady enough that they didn't shrivel during the brutal summers.

In the center of the courtyard was a large wooden worktable. She set the spray bottle down and snipped rosemary and peppermint from the planter boxes that lined the walls of the space. From a cedar cabinet near the door, she collected a jar full of sea salt, turned the knob that started the propane under her gas grill and took a cast iron Dutch oven from underneath. The water from the spray bottle went into the pot, followed by a handful of salt, some peppercorns, and the herbs.

It was absurd to the think a simple banishing spell would rid them of something like their mother's ghost- they'd never be that lucky-but it was a start.

She wiped a hand across her forehead, definitely feeling the heat that day. The courtyard seemed to tip to one side and she touched the grill cover to steady herself. *Wow, you are getting old.*

Normally, the cool breeze that swept across the back of her neck just then would have been more than welcome, except that it wasn't normal at all. When it was that hot in the desert, the wind blew hot as well. She inhaled deeply, and when she let out her breath, she could see it.

"Witch."

Laura felt the word as much as heard it, and the sensation made her shudder. She couldn't make herself face it just yet, so she took a handful of salt from the jar and whispered, "You're not welcome here."

"I was never, ever welcome here."

There was fury in her voice when Laura spun around. "If you thought that, then it's your own fault. You did it to yourself."

Brona was standing just inside the gate leading from the courtyard to the backyard and Laura wondered how a ghost could have opened it. It gave her little time to think about it as it ambled across the tiles, running a hand across the rosemary plant.

"Rosemary…rosemary is for remembrance…and for protection."

Laura stared in surprise that her mother would know such a thing.

The sprigs withered under Brona's touch. "I know more than you think, Sherlock." She seemed pleased with herself and lifted her chin defiantly; a gesture Laura had seen a million times.

Brona had taken to calling her Sherlock when she was about thirteen. It was an attempt to make Laura feel stupid, but since her mother wouldn't allow herself to utter the words, "no shit," she never quite got the insult right. Later in life, Laura started calling herself Sherlock whenever she made a mistake and often wondered how many hours of therapy it would take to sort that out.

"I don't know what you are, but I said you're not welcome here. Get out!"

She pitched the salt, and the spirit vanished as the white flakes rained down where it had been standing. Laura's breath escaped in loud gasps, and she leaned on the table to steady herself once again.

"You hungover, Auntie?"

Audi pushed through the open gate with Sarah at her heels, looking grim.

"She was here, wasn't she?" Sarah turned in anxious circles, looking for her mother.

Laura nodded and stumbled around a bit before taking a seat on a stool. The heat had overwhelmed her, and she put a hand to her mouth in disbelief of the entire experience.

Audi turned off the burner, then sought out a glass and a bottle of brandy. She put the drink in Laura's hand and did her own scan of the place.

"Uh, maybe some water, too," Sarah suggested, wondering what spell her daughter concocted that allowed her to instantly find the alcohol in everyone's house. She made a mental note to ask about it later and returned her focus to Laura. "Are you sure you're alright?"

"I think so. What could she possibly want now, Sarah? Is she really not done messing with us?"

Audi brought the water and returned to the grill. After sniffing the contents of the Dutch oven, she turned it back on, gave it a stir and whispered over the pot. The liquid bubbled up again and the scent of rosemary and peppermint wafted through the little courtyard.

That brew, when sprayed on the doors and windows would give her aunt some protection. If they were lucky, it would at least keep the horrid thing out of the house.

## Chapter Six

Sebastian's heart thumped loudly in his chest as he turned down Temecula Street. He hadn't spoken to Laura in over a month and was on his way to tell her about the problem with the Mercer family, telling himself she would want to know. Funny that it had seemed like a great idea when he left the office, but now he wasn't so sure.

His pulse quickened further as he pulled the white government issue Chevy pickup in front of her house. Laura's red Jeep Wrangler was parked in the driveway with a blue Cherokee next to it. *Great, Sarah, too.* Beads of sweat collected on his forehead, but he forced himself to get out and made his way up the terra cotta path.

"This will be quick," he said out loud to no one. "I just need to see her this once." His mouth dried out and his mind dragged him back to one of the memories he hated the most.

### *Six Weeks Earlier*

"Wait, are you saying you'd have to kill someone?" Bash and Laura were seated at a table for two in the back of Isaac's Oasis. While you could order food in either the front or the back of the place, the front was dedicated to families who would rather not have their kids exposed to pool sharks and bar fights.

Laura could remember Friday nights when moms would prop baby carriers right on the bar. They'd order beer and cheese sticks while waiting for their husbands to show up after work. She never had a husband, but Brian spent dozens of Fridays back there while she chatted with her friends at the bar. He'd learned to two-step and to play pool and he'd learned what to do when trouble showed up. In her opinion, it was actually more of a family friendly place back then.

"I'm saying if it is a werewolf, there's only one way to stop it." She leaned across the table and lowered her voice. "Right now, you've got a few dead animals, but pretty soon there will be missing children. We have to get rid of it before that happens." Her eyes brightened and she added with excitement, "I've never seen a werewolf."

He stared at her for a long minute, then pushed back in his chair, took a swig of beer and put the bottle to his forehead.

She swallowed hard. *Uh oh.*

They rode in silence when he took her home and the muscles in her chest contracted as the seed of heartache began to sprout. They'd been struggling for a while, so she knew what was coming next and that it was going to suck.

He walked her up the porch steps and she leaned against the door, folding her arms across her chest. "I take it you're not coming in?"

He sat on the bench swing and leaned forward, resting his elbows on his knees. "It's not that I don't believe in what's out there, Laura. I know what I've seen, and I know what you can do." He leaned back and folded his hands. "You're thinking we make this great team, but you operate in these messy, gray areas. You go to such dark places."

She put her hands on her hips. "I know you're not afraid of monsters, Sebastian, so what are you really trying to say?" She moved a hand to her chest. "Are...are you afraid of...me?"

He shook his head in frustration. "I'm not afraid of you, I'm afraid of losing you to all of this."

She laughed out loud. "That's rich, coming from a cop."

He looked at the ground. "I didn't say it was fair."

She blinked back tears. "Are you really doing this to us? I can't help it that the world isn't..." her voice trailed off.

"No, but you can control your actions. It's like you don't even care what I think."

"It's not about you, Sebastian. There are things out there that only I can deal with."

She could call him stupid and narrow minded, a coward even, but she didn't believe those things. He just didn't get it and she didn't understand why they couldn't work together.

"You don't think I'm incapable, and I'm not the only woman you've stood next to in battle."

"You're the one I'm falling in love with, dammit, and I don't know what to do." He ran a hand through his hair.

She was exasperated. "It's easy. We take care of each oth—" his cell phone rang before she could go any further.

"It's Chuck," he said, stepping off the porch to take the call.

Watching him pace the driveway as he talked, the ache in her chest swelled. If she was honest, he was probably right. She'd romanticized their future into a demented image of coffee and kisses and monsters and magic. Was it not more realistic that he would have to arrest her for arson or murder? And yeah, she could die. He was right about that, too.

He was no better for her. He'd fallen in love at nineteen but was deployed for most of his marriage and never truly got to know his wife or her family. When Sherry died in a car crash, he spent years trying to wrestle his daughter from his mother-in-law. No judge would give custody of a four-year-old girl to a military policeman stationed in the Middle East.

He knew everyone was just looking out for his little girl, but Sherry's family made sure that Becky didn't even know him for most of her childhood. What he was able to salvage of their relationship over the years amounted to nothing but awkward monthly phone calls and he hated them for that.

Bitterness made him a cold man, at least on the outside. Before he met Laura, he hadn't allowed a woman to so much as spend a whole night with him in years. He didn't want any more children, which complicated relationships in his thirties so he shut down that part of his heart. It worked so well for him that he continued the practice into his forties. You can't hurt anyone, or get hurt, if you keep everything casual.

She chuckled at the irony. In the end, he was letting his strong feelings for her ruin their relationship. She knew better than anyone else that fairy tales were just horror stories in disguise and mocked herself for thinking she had found something special that late in life.

He ended his call and interrupted her thoughts. "Jenny Mercer has gone missing. The family was picnicking at the new park, and they lost track of her this afternoon."

Laura dug a ponytail holder out of her pocket and began tying up her hair. "She's fifteen, right?"

"They're dragging the lake."

"I'm betting she's not in the lake."

"Laura…"

"The point that you keep missing is, whether we're together or not, I will help wherever I can," she said. "Don't worry about it, Sheriff. Just do your job and let me do mine."

"Where are you going?"

"Someplace dark," she snapped, "but I'll try not to make a mess." She jerked open the door of the Jeep and added, "God, I really thought you would be different."

He climbed into his truck and watched her wipe tears from her eyes. She preferred to have him at her side, but apparently, it was just his tough luck if he wasn't the man she'd thought he was. She would use her power however she wanted, with or without him. The magnitude of his mistake was beginning to settle over him, and he felt like shit.

The new park addition was right outside of town. He drove down Watkins Road past a troop of Boy Scouts camped out for the night and an unmanned Ranger Station before he found her Jeep.

When he caught up with her, she was crouched on one side of a mesquite tree just this side of the bridge over the man-made lake. She whipped around as he approached, pointing her tiny .38 Special in his face.

"Jesus Bash, I almost shot you."

"What are you doing?" he whispered.

"Well, it's a revenant, not a werewolf."

He blinked at her.

"Think ghost slash zombie."

He sighed. "Does it have Jenny?"

Laura pointed to a young girl laying in the ravine.

"It dropped her when I ran up on it. She's hurt but she'll be okay, at least physically."

His eyes narrowed. "Where is it?"

"Just under the bridge, right over the waterline. It would be better if my sister were here to help with her powers, but I'm going to light it up."

He touched her arm. "What do you need from me?"

She hesitated for a moment, then shoved a road flare at him. "Spark it when I tell you to."

An angry howl came from the brush under the bridge. They nodded to each other and made their way down through the brush toward the water, and toward the sound. It roared again and Bash thought of the Boy Scouts.

"I can't see it." Laura whispered. They kept their backs to the dirt wall so it couldn't get behind them so, naturally, it sprang from above.

"Christ!" Bash drew his gun as the thing landed on Laura, knocking her head against the ground. He fired three times, and it flew off of her as the bullets hit its body. The revenant was a man, or it once was, with much of his skin missing. The flesh around his collarbone and hips hung loose in chunks that slapped against his body.

"I need the flare!" she shouted.

He pulled the cap off and struck it across the ignitor, sparking a small flame from the top. She waved her hand at the flare and the flame stretched across the distance between them until it formed a ball between her hands. The revenant was on its feet, heading in their direction, so she raised her hands overhead and threw the fireball. When it hit the creature in the head, she spread her arms, widening it to a blanket of flame. The revenant screamed and lurched forward, but Bash emptied his revolver and it fell to its knees before it reached her. Laura moved closer, the flames intensifying with each of her steps until the being collapsed on its back. She lowered her hands, diminishing the flames enough for her to get on top of it.

She pulled a dagger from her jacket and attempted to stab the creature in the chest, but it writhed underneath her weight and clawed at her hands.

"The heart," she panted, "it has to come out."

Bash held it down with his knees and covered her hand with his own. Together, they dug through the fibrous tissues that held the heart. At last, Bash was able to shove his hand in and pull the organ from the revenant's chest cavity.

He dropped the heart next to them and flames followed Laura's hand across the revenant's body engulfing it. As its key organ blackened, the creature convulsed, and then stilled.

Laura sat back on her heels, exhausted, and Bash raised his cell phone to his ear.

"Yeah, tell them we found the girl and that I need an ambulance at the new lake."

"Bash," Laura gripped his hand when the paramedics loaded her in the ambulance. "Revenants don't just appear. Usually, they've been killed and they're looking for revenge. That girl wasn't a random choice. You could have a murder on your hands."

She lost consciousness at some point, but her wounds weren't debilitating – two stitches over her left eyebrow and a slight concussion.

The next day, Bash made a big deal in the emergency room about how a 'mountain lion' had been put down, knowing people would believe that story because it happened all the time. The residents of Chuparosa would believe the revenant story, too, but he saw no reason to stir them up. If Laura was right, and there was a murderer in town, the less that individual knew about last night, the better.

He was already regretting the things he'd said to her but wasn't quite able to navigate around his emotional firewall. Still, maybe there was a way he could protect her and his heart. Another officer had driven her Jeep to the hospital and outside, Bash ran his hand over the hood. He would come to regret quite a few things in the coming weeks.

* * *

No one answered the front door, so he went around the house to the back gate. The sound of Laura's voice stopped him in his tracks.

"I don't know, maybe she's not done torturing us."

"Or," Sarah's daughter offered, "Maybe Hell doesn't want her either."

Sarah sighed. "Audra, please."

The women stopped talking when they noticed him at the gate, taking in the scene. There was a lot of tension the air, but plenty of that was on him. He was the ex-boyfriend with the audacity to saunter up, unannounced. There was a shot glass in Laura's hand, even though it was still late in the morning. She was pale and shaking but tried to pull it together when she saw him. He clenched his jaw. *Things are very wrong here.*

The Chuparosa sheriff's department opted for a casual uniform. Bash wore faded jeans and a navy button-down shirt with "Sheriff's Department - Town of Chuparosa" embroidered on the pocket, sleeves rolled to his elbows, exposing his well-built forearms. His badge was clipped next to the side arm that hung from a leather holster on his belt and he carried his gray Stetson cowboy hat, turning it over in his hands as he stood in front of them.

His chocolate brown eyes had a mournful slope to them that gave people the impression he was a gentle man, despite his intimidating height and solid build. It was true that he had an empath's heart, but he was raised to have no outlet for those sensitivities. The softness of his eyes belied the resulting quick temper that simmered just below the surface of his good nature. Those who tested him were often caught off guard by how ferocious he could be in response.

For her part, Laura understood how much more than temper smoldered under that gaze. He could be rough and unreasonable, but no man had ever made her feel more special, at least for a while.

She recognized the concern as it crossed his face before he forced his expression back to neutral. Seeing him stand there sent fresh cracks through her heart, and Laura had to look away. She caught sight of her cut-off shorts and torn t-shirt, thinking, "I am twitchy and day drinking. Fabulous."

She rubbed her forehead. "Sarah, you remember Sebastian."

Sarah nodded and motioned toward Audi, who remained at the grill with her back to them.

"That's Audra, my daughter."

"Audi, this is Sheriff's Deputy Sebastian Scott," Laura said.

Audi turned her head and nodded, "We met a couple of times."

Sarah looked from her daughter to Bash. "Really?"

"Not a big deal." Audi gave Bash a threatening glare and reached toward the bottle of Brandy on the table. It hovered a moment, then floated across the courtyard to her hand. She put it back in the cabinet, grabbed a funnel and returned to her work.

"Got it." He put a finger to his lips and turned to the others. "Is everything okay here?"

Sarah smiled sweetly at him. "Our dead mother has been haunting us, and we're trying to figure out the best course of action moving forward."

He stared at her.

"But, what can we do to help *you*, Sheriff?"

He straightened his shoulders and faced Laura. "I came to say that you were right about the Mercers. I think the revenant was David Martin."

Her eyes widened.

He told them how Dotty Martin reported her husband, David, missing weeks ago.

"Since he was a grown ass man who tended to wander, no one took her seriously. That is, until it came out that he screwed over Bob Mercer on a construction site. Bob-you know, he's an unstable mother fucker-had about thirty witnesses who saw him at the Oasis, threatening to kill David and bury him in the park. Nobody thought anything of it, but Chuck and I went to the park to check it out. Sure enough, we found a shallow pit about a quarter of a mile from the bridge that just might have been a grave."

His voice was telling the story, but his eyes were focused on Laura. She was barefoot, wearing cutoff jean shorts and a worn, white, long-sleeved Duran Duran concert t-shirt. A silver pentacle dangled from a leather cord around her neck and her chestnut-colored hair hung long and straight down her back with a few strands draping over her collar bone. Narrow streaks of white wove their way in and out of a small section she'd braided on one side. He recalled those bare legs wrapped around his middle and stammered through the end of his story.

"Any, uh, anyway, we figure the revenant who took Jenny Mercer was David. You, uh, said revenants were vengeful spirits, so he likely took her to punish Bob for killing him. Sacks of shit, both of them, if you ask me. Of course, we can't prove anything without a body but…"

He ran a hand through his hair again. *Get it together.* "I'm sorry, did you say your mother is haunting you?"

Laura nodded. "Her passing is, apparently, still pending and we're trying to figure out how to move things along."

"If she hadn't been cremated, we could dig up her bones and burn them," Sarah offered.

Audi rolled her eyes "Okay, Dean Winchester."

Sarah sighed and leaned against a planter. "I know he's not real, but wow."

Laura smirked. "We could turn her ashes into incense and sell it at market day."

Bash looked from woman to woman, unsure of what to say next, but very sure he was out of his depth. He knew of course, but Laura had never told him her mother died. That stung, but why would she? Like an asshole, he hadn't reached out to her about it either. He knew he was lucky she didn't carbonize him when he walked through the gate, so he needed to wrap up his visit, no matter how good she looked. *No matter how much he missed her.*

Audi piped up from the grill. "Bob Mercer is a loudmouth, but do you really think he could be a murderer?"

Laura's shoulders sagged. "I torched your evidence, Bash. Without a body, could Bob get away with it?"

He shrugged. "I have a few ideas and I'll keep you posted. I just thought you'd want to know the whole story."

Sarah batted her eyelashes, "Anything else, Officer?"

He squirmed. "That's it. Laura it was, uh, good to see you. Audi, stay out of trouble."

She gave him the peace sign with two fingers.

He touched the brim of his hat and said, "Sarah, always a pleasure," as he turned to leave.

When he was clear of the courtyard, Audi stomped to the gate and gave it a long spray with the seasoned water. "Talk about a meeting that could have been an email," she scoffed. "We should have hexed him to be allergic to beer."

Sarah laughed and put her hand over Laura's. "Someone appears to be rethinking his life choices."

## Chapter Seven

They took Laura's Wrangler to the cemetery so Audi could practice driving a stick shift and Sarah held on tightly in the back seat.

"I don't know how you tolerate all of this bouncing around. It is the most unstable ride."

Audi giggled. "Maybe it reminds her of her love life."

Laura furrowed her brow. "That's hilarious. Pay attention to the road."

As they approached the cemetery, Audi complained, "I don't get why we have to meet here."

"We're checking the gravesites." Sarah explained. "If they've been disturbed, we might not be dealing with an actual ghost."

"Necromancy?" Laura wondered, "On ashes?"

Kevin was buried in the Chuparosa Cemetery and after Brona's cremation, they buried her ashes next to him. A new headstone had been ordered that said simply, 'United.' It was a secret jab from their daughters with a nod to the pretense their parents presented to the church and all of their friends.

Drew waited at the gravesite, smiling to himself as they approached. It was like a Miss Clairol commercial coming straight for him. Each woman was tall, but Audi had at least two inches on the others. She featured her father's brown skin and soft jawline, but the Deane temperament was undeniably on display. That day, her t-shirt read, "It's a good day to destroy the patriarchy".

He didn't worry about her, not yet anyway. As soon as she had displayed her gifts, Sarah and Laura taught her how and when to use them. She was always along for the ride and he suspected it was as much to keep an eye out for them as it was to learn her craft.

He did worry about the other two. They thought they'd escaped a lifetime of mental torture when Brona died. What was the haunting going to do to them? Even worse, what if he was right and they'd done this to themselves?

His back straightened as they got closer. They had never cast a single spell in his direction, but he was utterly bewitched.

Laura's long hair shown copper in the sun. She wore a sage green, ruffle hem smock dress with a denim jacket over it and a jade butterfly hung from a gold chain deep in the v-neckline. He'd heard her described harshly, but it was a bad idea to mistake her sensitive nature for fragility. What others might call unbalanced, he called insightful, and he adored her for it. Her sunglasses hid vivid green eyes that, along with the warmth of her smile could probably stop traffic with no magic necessary. As far as she was concerned, he and his church were on perpetual probation, but she never treated him with anything other than genuine kindness.

He knew better, but his gaze always settled on Sarah. Her hair was much darker than her sister's, swept into a loose bun at the nape of her neck on that day. She was wearing blue jeans with a white, eyelet lace top. He thought her more subdued, perhaps even classier than the other two. It was only her ice blue eyes that hinted at how dangerous she could be.

He called on her family one night after Brona went into the hospital. Audi was in class and Rueben, while polite, was never interested in company. She gave him a beer and they sat talking on the back porch.

She revealed her powers when, being so tall, he knocked the hummingbird feeder off its nail, and she caught it mid-air with her mind. She positioned herself in front of him as he rehung the feeder and touched his face. Searching his eyes for judgment and finding none, she issued him a silent plea for sanctuary with a warning of the risk involved if he gave it. The bizarre exchange was over in moments, but it was the most intimate and unnerving experience he'd ever shared with another human being, and he thought about it every day.

He was heartened by her trust in him. Their early experiences in the church were kindred, and maybe she sensed that in him from the beginning. He had been punished severely for questioning the rules and for doubts he wrestled with still.

The Deane women, who never changed their names for marriage, not even Brona, wore their powers lightly but he knew if provoked, they could be deadly. They were dangerous, but he wasn't afraid. It was as if they were part of something remarkable that he was supposed to do with his life and he would never turn his back on them.

They'd been laughing at something, but stopped short when they saw him, their faces suddenly devoid of emotion. They closed ranks out of caution and he wasn't part of their inner circle, though he longed for that to change.

Someone had put flowers on Brona's side of the grave, and Sarah swiped a carnation out of the vase. "Are you satisfied that no one has tampered with the grave?" She plucked off the petals one by one and tossed them away.

"I am, and that has me worried." He moved closer to them. "You've cleansed your houses, you've intensified your wards, and you're still 'haunted'. He made air quotes with his hands.

"Why do you say 'haunted' like that?" Audi asked, making her own air quotes.

He sat them on some benches under a tree. "The spiritual realm is very real, even though most people can't see it. From time to time though, God will let some people, like you, in."

Laura raised her eyebrows. "Freaks like us?"

Sarah rolled her eyes. "Laura's right. Lots of people see ghosts. We're witches, we're not special."

Drew turned to her. "I saw it at your house, and it was no ghost. It had form, and it moved quickly." He blew out a deep breath before asking, "Have you ever heard of a rage demon?"

They gaped at him.

"Yes, a rage demon. I think you created it."

Laura put her hands up. "I'm at least eighty percent sure I've never summoned a demon."

"Hear me out," he continued, "Carl Jung believed that personal shadow-demons rest inside everyone's sub-conscience. The shadow is the self we hide from the world, and it includes the rage and anger we repress, the trauma we've suffered. In most people, it manifests in some sort of mental illness or anxiety. It could be nightmares about seeing a monster in a mirror, or being chased down a never-ending hallway by a devil that looks like someone you know."

Laura stopped him. "No, sir. Shadow work is about getting comfortable with the hateful parts of yourself that you don't want anyone to see. I've been doing that work for years. You can't truly love yourself until you can accept your shadow, blah, blah, blah. That has nothing to do with ghosts."

Sarah pulled her sunglasses down her nose. "Andrew, are you suggesting that we need therapy?"

He shook his head. "Think about it. How socially acceptable is it to hate your mother, to really hate your mother? Mothers are some of the most exalted women in our society. How long ago did you start to swallow your feelings about her? These shadows are born out of guilt, shame, and pain. Was your mother not doling out those emotions, in spades, until the very end of her life? You were deeply traumatized by that woman, and you are magical people. It makes sense that your trauma would manifest itself in a more tangible form."

Audi nodded. "Like, Build-A-Bear, but make it a demon."

He slapped his knee. "Yes, exactly. You see your mother, but that's not what I saw."

Laura took a step back. "If that's true, you need to stay away from us. Far, far away."

Sarah nodded. "It knows you now, and that's not good."

"No, please don't shut me out, let me do some more research. Are you kidding? Seeing that thing in your house has honestly given my faith a bit of a boost. If that kind of evil can exist, then something to counter it must also exist."

"Sweet summer child," Audi murmured.

"Listen, I can't get rid of it for you, but let me help you."

Sarah took his hands in hers. "Please be careful."

They were interrupted by the sound of a pickup as it turned around on the main cemetery road and Laura's eyes narrowed when she recognized the sheriff's logo on the side.

That was not the first time Bash had appeared in a random location of hers since they broke up. She would have thought a stalker would be more menacing. At the very least, a lifelong cop should be stealthier. Why was he watching her anyway? *He* broke up with *her*. Whatever he was trying to do, he was terrible at it but even so, it pissed her off.

She gazed into the sky and back at the others. "Have you noticed an awful lot of crossover from the Other Side lately? Goblins? Revenants? Now we've got a demon. Since when are we combat witches? I mean, I make herbal tea."

She stared down at her mother's grave for a few moments, then kicked over the vase of flowers and turned to leave.

When they approached the Jeep, Laura stopped Audi from climbing inside.

"Hang on." She dropped to the ground and scooted underneath. "That asshole." She pushed herself out holding a small electronic device in her hand.

Drew cringed and unlocked his 4Runner, "I'll be in touch." *Rest in peace, Sebastian*, he added to himself.

A brooding, long-haired figure stood under a nearby Cottonwood tree and pressed his fingers together. The German Shepherd looked up at him and snarled.

## Chapter Eight

Bash was at his desk Googling "Dean Winchester" when his phone chimed with a notification from the GPS tracker in Laura's Jeep. He'd thought he could keep an eye on her from a distance, be there if she needed him, but not emotionally involved. *Emotionally at risk.*

It hadn't been often, but each time he followed her, waves of self-loathing flowed through him and when he saw her earlier at the cemetery, he knew he would never use the tracker again.

"I thought you got enough supernatural in your day to day, man," Chuck looked over his shoulder at the computer screen.

Bash closed the browser. "I told you; we broke up."

Chuck Ruiz sat in the guest chair and propped his feet on Bash's desk. "I think you forgot to tell yourself."

Bash joined the County Sheriff's Department after retiring from the Army and had worked with Chuck off and on for almost ten years. He'd received the 'military or prison' speech in a grubby Juvenile courtroom in

Phoenix when he was seventeen years old. The judge had also once been an angry, fatherless boy and frequently used the bench to reach kids like Sebastian before their petty crimes became felonies. Chuck didn't know him back then, but suspected all those years in and out of the Middle East might have actually saved his friend's life.

As a child, Chuck travelled from Mexico with his parents every year and he would never have dared to get in the kind of trouble Bash did as a teenager. Risking his family's future like that would have been unthinkable.

Bash struggled when he started with the department in downtown Phoenix, and often volunteered for obscure assignments to get away from the big city politics, befriending Chuck along the way. Chuck asked him more than once to join him in Chuparosa and one day out of the blue, he received the call.

Bash said, "Hey man, do you still need help watching the paint dry out there?"

In high school, Chuck fell in love with Jimena Marquez and Laura was her protective best friend. He ended up liking the Deane sisters very much, which was a good thing because when he married Mena, they came as a package deal. He was there when Bash met Laura and thought-hoped-it would be a slam dunk for them.


**_Eight months earlier_**

The deputies were on an animal control call that night and Bash was annoyed.

"This is bullshit," he complained. "Where's county?"

Chuck dug around in the truck's toolbox. "This is the wild west, my friend. County don't care about us. Besides, what else were you gonna do?" He handed Bash a pair of gloves and a leash pole.

"This is bullshit." Bash repeated, flicking on his headlamp.

About a hundred yards into their patrol, something crossed their path. "Bingo."

There was a crash and a squeal behind them. "Oh, great," Chuck grumbled, "there's more than one."

Bash tapped Chuck's arm and pointed. "Look right there, what the hell is that?"

It was about four feet tall, with a chubby torso. At first, it scurried on all fours, but it stood when it saw them and ran off on two legs.

"Did something escape the zoo?"

They started after it, but a woman jumped in front of them. "Watch it!" She held her arms out wide to keep them back.

She ignited a small kitchen torch then dropped it, keeping the flame in her hand. Bash and Chuck snuck behind the creature and the woman stretched the flame between her fingers like a Chinese jump rope. It noticed the men coming from behind and stepped closer to her.

"That's right," she taunted, "come here, creepy."

Bash took a step forward. "What is she doing?"

Chuck held him back. "She's alright, just don't let it get away."

The woman straightened her arms and tossed the flame strings around the creature like a ribbon, crossed her arms in front of her and then spread them wide. It shrieked and screamed as the flames sliced through, and it fell to ashes at her feet.

The men raced after another creature that scurried behind them into a dry wash but lost sight of it in the brush. Bash drew his gun and turned in careful circles as he searched, but it lunged out of the darkness and whacked him in the head with a large tree branch.

Chuck fired, but yet another one knocked the gun out of his hand. Both creatures made their way toward Bash, who laid motionless in the dirt. Chuck stepped defensively in front of his friend and called for Laura. Bash sat up just as she slid down the embankment, slamming her body into one of the creatures and sending it flying into a tree trunk.

She grabbed hold of the branch it used to beat Bash and shoved it into its belly, loosening its grip. It bit down on her arm, and though she cried out, she was able to wrestle the branch away, swinging it like a baseball bat as hard as she could, knocking the creature's head clean off.

She gave the branch to Chuck and stuck her hand out to Bash, leaning into her heels to haul him to his feet. She reached up and touched where the blood was running from his bottom lip along his jaw.

"You okay?"

"I think so." He nodded at her arm, "You?"

She looked down and made a face. "Probably."

Chuck kept his eyes on the ground, searching for his gun, but pointed roughly in her direction.

"This is Laura Deane."

Bash swallowed hard. *Laura.*

She sighed, "We got goblins again, Chuck."

"Aw, hell."

"Goblins?" Bash blinked at her. "Again?"

"Flimsy little bastards." She gestured to the severed head on the ground at their feet. "But they travel in packs."

She dug a roll of gauze from a small pouch on her hip, tore some off and handed the rest to Bash. She lightly pressed the cloth to the cut on his jaw, then pulled some ointment from her pouch.

"Hold still." He did as he was told while she dabbed it on his busted lip.

When she was done, he unrolled the rest of the gauze around the now oozing bite on her arm. He was a big man and his grip was strong, but he was gentle with her. She marveled that though he'd nearly had his brains bashed in, his hands were steady. He smelled of sweat, dirt, and Irish Spring, and she found herself taking several long, deep breaths.

He gave her a warm, but worried smile. "Are you gonna turn into one of those things?"

She twisted her mouth in thought. "As far as I know, a goblin's bite isn't infectious."

"As far as you know?"

Another woman then made her way down the embankment. "Where's the last one? Hey Chuck, how's it going?" She looked Bash up and down. "Who are you?"

Chuck picked up his gun. "This is Sebastian Scott, the new deputy."

Laura bit her bottom lip and Sarah rolled her eyes.

Chuck waved at the top of the wash and as the women made their way up, Bash cornered him.

"You never thought to tell me about the goblins? More importantly, you never thought to mention the lovely goblin hunter?"

Chuck sighed. "We haven't had much real trouble with the Other Side in a few years. If we don't take them down, they'll start stealing pets and babies. Laura and Sarah are witches, so it makes sense that they would be out here. Laura probably called the 'loose animal' into dispatch. She thinks she's funny."

"Witches? How do you know witches?"

"We went to high school together."

Bash ran a hand through his hair. "Jesus, this town."

The four of them turned off their flashlights and crossed the field using the full moon to guide them. After fifty yards or so, Chuck gave a low whistle, and they closed ranks. The goblin was sitting under a mesquite tree right in front of them, chewing on a jackrabbit. It sniffed the air and, dropping the rabbit, bolted past them.

Bash took off after it and the others fanned around the field in a circle to keep it from getting away. Bash was gaining, but he wouldn't be able to catch it. Then, the goblin changed their luck by looking over its shoulder and stumbling around a low bush. Bash dropped to the ground and slid across the dirt kicking its feet out from under it. It squirmed and gnashed its teeth, but he held tight to the legs, giving Chuck time to take a shot. When it quit squirming, Bash pushed the dead thing off of him, rolled onto his back, and groaned.

Chuck knelt beside him, grinning. "You okay old man? Did you just break your hip trying to impress her?"

"Shut up."

"Wow," Laura said, not taking her eyes off of Sebastian, "do you think he's alright?"

"Good god, you're drooling."

They gathered and piled the goblin bodies in the wash so Laura could incinerate them while Chuck did some more explaining for Bash's benefit.

"Most of the town has encountered something from the Other Side at some point, but there's no reason to cause a stir."

Bash crossed his arms. "Of course not."

They put the fire out with water from the truck and walked the women to their Jeep.

Sarah tugged on Chuck as he took out his phone. "If you're calling Mena, tell her we'll see her at Isaac's on Tuesday night." He nodded and held up his hand.

Laura gave Bash a wry smile and touched his arm. "Nice job out there tonight."

She'd been so tough in the fight, but so achingly tender with him and he already liked her very much. It was disarming to a man who usually kept his feelings firmly guarded, so he overcompensated by feigned aloofness. It would keep him awake cursing himself for many nights after that, but the only response he could manage was a terse, "Take care."

He feared she'd never speak to him again after that, and he never dreamed she would end up loving him like no one ever had.

As the women pulled away, Chuck took a notepad out of the glove box and wrote something down. When he hung up, Bash wondered, "Are you actually reporting the goblins?"

"Nope." Chucked ripped off the page and handed it to him.

"What's this then?"

"Her number."

* * *

"What have you got there?" Chuck snatched up Bash's phone from the desk.

"Nothing."

"You're not on surveillance, who are you tracking? He looked closer, incredulous. "Are you crazy, man?"

Bash sat back in his chair. "It's not like that."

"It sure as hell looks like that." Chuck leaned in and lowered his voice. "You are a Deputy god damned Sheriff."

Bash rubbed his eyes. "I know, I know. It's not what you think. I'm getting rid of it."

"You better. Look, your heart is in the right place, but you're a mess." Chuck waved the phone in the air. "This ain't the way. Why don't you try to work on a different reality? One where for some reason, she puts up with you."

"Do you think she would even consider that at this point?"

They heard the Wrangler's tires screeching to a stop in front of the station and jumped to their feet. Laura threw the Jeep in park and hopped out.

Audi grinned at her mother and leaned over the dash to better see inside the building. "We're definitely getting some wine on the way home."

Laura threw open the glass door. "Sebastian!" All five men in the station hit the floor as she wound up and threw the GPS tracker as hard as she could. "You stalking mother fucker!"

"Argh!" The device hit Bash on the side of the head and bounced on the tile next to Chuck. With both hands, she shoved the papers on his desk to the floor, flipped him the bird and stormed out the door.

As the others stood up, they didn't even try to hide their laughter, doubling over and holding onto the walls.

Chuck tossed the tracker to Bash. "I guess sometimes life's questions have a way of answering themselves."

## *Chapter Nine*

The St. Patrick's Day party at Isaac's Oasis was legendary in Chuparosa and drew nearly everyone in town. The afternoon started with face painting, scavenger hunts and bounce houses for the kids, then segued into a barbecue at night.

Isaac hired a DJ and extra bartenders and hauled out an enormous dance floor, built years ago specifically for the event. March usually meant the end of the cooler weather and most of Arizona was braced for the sweltering summer, so it was the perfect time for everyone to be outside.

Sarah, Rueben, Laura, Chuck, and Mena sat outside at a large round table decorated with green and silver balloons. They were laughing and watching Brian, Audi, and Tina Ruiz play pool through the bar's open side windows.

Audi and Tina had recently developed an obsession with Southern Gothic style and wore matching black ankle-length ruffled skirts. Audi's lavender cap sleeved t-shirt said "Creepy Ain't a Crime".

Tina opted for a black peasant blouse and they both wore wide leather belts and cowboy boots. A long strand of amethyst beads around Audi's neck dragged the pool table as she lined up her shot.

Mena leaned over Chuck to talk in Laura's ear. "Chuck said Bash is following up some leads on the Mercer case and that's why he's not here."

Laura shrugged.

"I call bullshit," Mena continued. "If he really wanted to break up with you, why was he stalking you? I bet he's afraid to see you right now because he knows you're pissed off. Chuck says Bash just wants to protect you, but he always goes about things the wrong way. I say, if he wanted to protect you, why would he leave you? I don't know what his problem is."

Sarah leaned over Mena, "Whatever. If he'd rather be miserable, then fine."

Laura picked up her drink. "I think the man's point was that I made him miserable, so..."

"No way!" the other two women shouted in unison.

Chuck extracted himself from between them and moved to a chair across the table.

Rueben laughed. "I thought you were a goner."

Laura sat back and sipped her Guinness. She was glad Bash had decided to stay away, whatever the reason. Getting over him was hard enough without running into him everywhere and she was still furious about the tracker too.

He wasn't a stalker, and he would beat the shit out of anyone else who did that, so what in the world was he thinking? Drilling it into the side of his head like a fastball probably wasn't the best way to find out, but she had no regrets about that.

The DJ was doing a great job with an eclectic mix of eighties pop and Sarah was bouncing in her chair. She loved to dance but it was always a hard 'no' from Rueben. Footloose came on and Chuck led Mena to the dance floor, and sensing Sarah's eyes on him, Rueben got up for another round. She sighed and rubbed at the back of her neck.

Laura took another sip. "What's that about?"

Sarah lowered her voice. "Audi was at school last night and, I wanted some attention, but…" she shook her head and thumbed over her shoulder in Rueben's direction, "So, I started rage cleaning, slamming doors and drawers and dishes-you know?"

Laura nodded.

"I dragged the vacuum out of the closet, tossed my hair out of the way, and slammed the door. When I bent down to unwrap the cord, my hair was caught in the god damned door."

Laura sniffed beer foam up her nose and choked out a guffaw.

"My head snapped backward, and I wrenched my neck."

"Oh, my God, stop, I can't." Laura wiped tears of laughter from her eyes.

"It's not funny. You know, he never even woke up?"

Drew had arrived and was getting ready to take a seat next to them, but stopped himself, having accidentally overheard their conversation. He looked from Sarah to Rueben in utter astonishment.

"Normally, I just let things go," Sarah added, "I mean, it could always be worse, right? But I'm really getting sick of it."

Laura thought for a minute before she spoke, "It's about time, you know."

Rueben returned and dropped off two beers. "Oh, hey man, I didn't know you were here, or I would have grabbed another one."

Drew shook his head and held up a hand as if to say, "No worries."

"I'm taking off," Rueben said to his wife.

"What? It's still so early-are you alright?"

"Yeah. Just a headache, I hate this music. Can you give her a ride home?"

Laura nodded but glared at him. The whole bar would be watching him walk away. *Crap. They will be talking about this for days.*

Brian had been watching from inside and when Rueben cleared the area, he handed his cue to Audi.

"Hey Auntie, let's dance." He led Sarah to the floor, passing Chuck and Mena on their way back to the table.

"Laura," Chuck said, "you raised that boy right."

Audi sauntered over and took her dad's empty seat next to Laura. She pointed to the pool table inside. "Your son owes me four million dollars."

There was a makeshift bar set up near the dance floor and next to it was a small table for two. A man sat there alone, nursing a highball of some sort with his gaze fixed on Laura.

Mena leaned over her husband and tapped Laura's arm, raising her eyebrows in the direction of the strange man.

Drew looked over his shoulder and back to Laura. "Do you know him?"

She shook her head. "He looks familiar though."

Mena whispered in Chuck's ear, and he patted her leg. "Don't worry, I see him."

Brian and Sarah finished their dance with him feigning exhaustion. "She wore me out!"

Audi sniffed. "The first rule is cardio."

"Hey man," Brian said to Drew, "do you want to play darts?"

They went inside and Sarah waved her hand across the table. "Another round?"

"I'm good, driving later," Chuck declined and left for the bathroom.

The man stood and met at the bar. "After you," he said.

While she waited for their drinks, he put his hand on her forearm and leaned in close to her. "I'd like to introduce myself."

He clenched her wrist when she tried to move her arm away. His grip was tight and painful, but an extraordinary surge of energy went through her body when he touched her.

At the table, Laura nudged Audi and Mena.

The man whispered to Sarah, "Don't you have a kiss for Daddy?"

He expected her to draw her arm back, and he was prepared to pull her in close, but she surprised him and jerked her arm straight down. His upper body followed, and she buried her other elbow into the side of his face just as Laura kicked in the back of his knees, forcing him to the ground. He tried to get up, but Laura stood on his calf, and Mena grabbed his ear while Audi pushed the end of a broken beer bottle to his neck.

"It's the shrimp-dick energy for me," Audi sneered.

A young man hollered, "Hey Brian, your Mom is beating the crap out of some dude by the bar!"

Chuck emerged from the bathroom in time to see Audi push the broken glass a little farther into the man's skin.

"Holy shit!" He ran to the bar and took what was left of the bottle from the girl. "Mena! Laura, get back!"

Out of nowhere, Brian grabbed the man by the collar, dragged him to his feet and shoved him against the bar. He looked Brian in the eyes and gave him a wicked grin. "You, sir, are very interesting." His gaze traveled to Laura. "This whole family is chock full of secrets."

Chuck took Brian by the shoulder and pulled him away. "Everybody just calm the fuck down!" Mena crossed her arms and raised her eyebrows at her husband as if to say, "You weren't watching very well, were you?"

A thin line of blood trickled down the man's neck, so Chuck held out a napkin. "Do you need medical attention?"

The man wiped the blood with the back of his hand and looked to Laura and Sarah. "No, I got what I came for. You are more than I expected, more than I could have hoped for even. A very, very pleasant surprise."

Laura noticed the German Shepherd sitting outside the fence and whispered to Sarah, "The guy from the trail."

Sarah leaned in close to his face. "Who are you?"

Chuck pulled her back and took the man by the arm. A wave of nausea rolled through him when they touched. "Let's go. We need to talk."

The man wrested away from Chuck and whistled, then the dog jumped over the fence and charged at Chuck. Mena screamed and it turned on her, teeth bared.

"Be still, honey."

"Hey!" Laura called to the dog and held out her hand. It started toward her, but another whistle travelled over the air. The dog snapped at the crowd and jumped over the fence. When they looked around, both he and the man were gone.

Audi let her head fall back. "Wonderful."

Isaac waved his hand at the DJ, who pumped the music louder and turned the strobe lights on. It was getting darker, and the onlookers were getting drunker.

"At least we have that going for us," Chuck thought.

The Phoenix-based bartender never had a gig with deadly chicks and invisible men before. He wished he'd had the sense to pull out his phone to record but had been too engrossed in the action. No one would believe it, but he intended to work the west side whenever he could from then on.

Mena snapped her fingers at him, barking, "Ice!", so he scooped some into a towel and handed it to her, then she shooed him away and put the towel on Sarah's wrist.

* * *

The young coyote had been standing on the side of the road for several minutes when it saw Bash's headlights heading toward him. As a rule, he would have instinctively withdrawn to the shadows, but the ground squirrel he was hunting earlier popped out of a hole and ran across the road.

Bash swerved to the shoulder as the coyote darted in front of his truck. "Jesus!" He hit the brakes just before careening into the canal that ran parallel to the road.

The coyote stood in front of the truck, ears back, peering at Bash in annoyance. The ground squirrel was long gone.

"You almost killed us both, buddy," Bash scolded him, and pulled back onto the road.

Before the reckless coyote incident, he'd been thinking about something Bob Mercer said at the hospital the night he and Laura killed the revenant. The doctor told Bob to take Jenny to a therapist. Being attacked by a wild animal would surely be traumatic for anyone, let alone a fifteen-year-old girl.

Bob told the doctor, "I only take assignments from one person."

At the time it seemed like the kind of thing any stubborn, unprogressive man would say. *No therapist necessary, Doctor. We have God for such things.*

The longer Bash thought about it, the more it didn't sit right with him. Bob Mercer was about as God fearing as he was, so who was he taking assignments from?

The Mercers lived about two miles outside of town in a five-bedroom ranch. Bash surveyed the area as he pulled into the circular driveway. It wasn't that late, but all the lights in the house were out. Chuck texted earlier that the Mercer's weren't at Isaac's party, so where was everyone? The garage door was open, and the light was on, so he got out and walked over. He thought he saw an enormous German Shepherd run past the side of the house, but he didn't remember them having a dog like that.

Bob was pacing the garage and muttering to himself so Bash put on his 'good old boy' charm and called out, "Hey Bob, how's it goin'?" He also rested his hand on his sidearm.

Bob whirled around, but relaxed a bit when he recognized Bash. "Hey Sheriff, I-I thought you were someone else."

"Oh yeah?" Bash looked around and squared his shoulders. "You expectin' company?"

"No, no, I guess not."

Like many American garages, Bob's housed no cars. A table saw, a drill press, and a grinder were arranged in one corner. Tools of all kinds hung from peg boards lining the walls, and a shop vac sat next to a work bench in the middle of the room.

Bash approached the bench and noted Bob had a buck knife, a K-Bar, a double-edged Gerber, and a handful of box cutters laid out. He picked up the K-Bar and raised his eyebrows.

"You know how it is," Bob laughed, "gotta keep everything maintained."

Bash put down the knife and positioned himself in front of the weapons. "So, you didn't go to the party?"

"No, no. I've got way too much to do."

"Like sharpening your knives?"

"I'm very busy, Sheriff."

Bash put up his hands. "I hear that." He moved a little closer. "Where's Connie? Jenny?"

Bob backed away from him. "They went to Tucson. Connie's sister is getting ready to have the baby. Look, like I said, I'm busy. Do you need something in particular?"

"No, no, just checkin' in. I wanted to see how everyone is doing after the—"

"Everyone is fine, just fine," Bob interrupted.

"Glad to hear it. I'll see you later." Bash left and radioed the Tucson office from his truck.

## Chapter Ten

Later that night, Laura settled in at the kitchen table putting together an order for the Wishing Tree shop. The nighttime tea she called, 'Dreamy' sold particularly well up there. Rhonda's recipe for stress relief was another hit that Laura called, 'Easy'. She couldn't imagine what people in Flagstaff had to worry about up in all those peaceful pines, far away from the heat and the rush of Phoenix.

She wasn't complaining though, and those teas were her best sellers everywhere. She included a new recipe with the order that she called, 'Busy', which was quite a bit more stimulating than the others.

Brian sat across the table filling cellophane bags with the herbs she measured out.

"Remember to keep your intention focused on providing calm to others," she coached.

He rolled his eyes. "I can't do what you do."

"The true power is in your intention and everything else is extra."

He looked down. "Speaking of intention, I'm not going back to school."

She dropped her scoop on the table. "Excuse me?"

"Things are way too weird right now. There's too much happening here in town."

She leaned back and rubbed her eyes. He wasn't wrong. Their list of issues was growing by the day, but one by one, she broke them down for him.

"Look, Pastor Drew will help me and Sarah get rid of Grandma. We have dealt with creepy guys our whole lives, and the one with the dog is no different. Things didn't work out with Bash—it happens. You've had breakups before, so you know how it is. It will all be back to normal by the time you're home for the summer and we'll go on vacation. If this order does well, I'll take you to New York."

"Stop treating me like a seven-year-old."

"I promise I will call you if we can't handle it."

"How will you know you can't handle it before it's too late?"

"Honey, what I know is that your future doesn't have to be caught up in all of this."

Brian slapped the counter. "Like Audi's?"

Until that moment, Laura had never been sure if Brian was resentful of Audi's powers, so she chose her next words carefully. "Audi doesn't get a choice."

The three-hour drive home from Flagstaff was always torture for Laura. She had Sarah, Audi, her friends, and her tea company, but it had been Brian and her against the world for eighteen years and she missed him terribly. She'd be lying though, if she said dropping him off at the dorm wasn't a relief this time. She was grateful that the only powers he displayed were in athletics and math so he could be a normal kid.

Her own college ambitions were thwarted early on. She wasn't a great student and certainly not bound for a traditional college like her sister, but she *was* Irish American. The Board of the Young Irish Fellowship in Phoenix loved her essay on the Cait Sidhe and the stray she'd taken care of for years. They gave her a five-hundred-dollar scholarship to put toward classes at the community college.

When it came time to register for her first semester, the check hadn't arrived, so she called the Fellowship office and they confirmed that they'd mailed it weeks earlier. Knowing the answer, she asked Brona about it several times, but her mother became more and more agitated with each question.

Finally, she shouted, "Leave me alone about the stupid money!"

Fury burned through Laura, and she advanced on her mother for the first time in her life. "What did you do? That check was made out to me."

Brona knew that Laura's powers had grown stronger and feared that she might have gone too far but rather than apologize, she doubled down, shouting, "Stay away from me, you selfish brat! You owe me anyway."

"It was for college!" Laura cried. "I was counting on that money!"

"Well, I was counting on a lot of things, too. Wake up, Sherlock. Sometimes we don't get what we want, so just get over it."

"I hate you! I hate you!" Laura screamed. She raised her arms and wind whipped through the kitchen where they stood, the toaster rose off the counter and the curtains blew into knots.

Brona shook her by the shoulders. "You monster! You're the devil!" The knobs on the stove turned and flames rose from the burners.

Brona screamed, "Stop it right now! You didn't deserve that money and you know it! It wasn't even for a real school!"

Rage rolled through Laura and wrapped around her like a shield. She reached out toward the stove and the flames rose to the ceiling.

Brona pushed her against the wall. "Stop it now, you ungrateful little bitch!"

Laura gave everything to her mother. Was it so wrong to want something for herself? Sarah was on track for a full ride to a state school, but that was never in the cards for Laura. She didn't even know what she wanted to study. As her confidence waned, the flames lowered and finally, the toaster fell back to the counter and Laura collapsed on the floor.

Brona stepped over her, hissing, "You make me sick."

Laura shifted in her seat as the unpleasant memory wound its way through her mind. She liked to stop outside of Black Canyon City for blueberry pie at her favorite roadside café and cheered up a bit as she approached the exit on I-17. Looking in the review mirror to change lanes, she spotted Brona glaring at her from the back seat and swerved off the road.

"You thought you were so smart," Brona sneered.

"Leave me alone."

"You're the oldest, but you were the always the weakest and you know that."

Laura unclipped her seat belt, took the lighter out of the center console and flicked the wheel. Just as she pushed her hand over the flame and sent a stream of fire into the back seat, the Brona demon opened the door and ran away.

Laura slapped the remaining fire out with her hand and rested her head on the steering wheel letting the sobs pour out of her. After ten minutes or so, she collected herself and continued to the café. She wasn't leaving without pie.

* * *

In Sarah's nightmare, she was in Mr. Reaver's truck, and he had his hand on her thigh. The Reavers lived just down the street, but he always insisted on driving her home after she babysat for them. He was already drunk when he and his wife returned from their date, but he grabbed another beer from the refrigerator before lifting Sarah into his truck.

Laura had warned her about him, so she was ready if he tried anything. They stopped asking her sister to sit when she turned thirteen, but Sarah was twelve then, just his type. He seemed harmless enough at first, but he drove slowly, rambling on about brunettes having the most fun.

He moved his hand from her thigh, flipped her ponytail through his fingers, and rested his arm around her neck. As his hand slipped below collar bone, she focused her intention on the beer bottle in his lap. The liquid bubbled up slowly at first, but as his fingers dipped lower, it overflowed into his lap, soaking his jeans.

"Shit!" He slammed on the brakes and grabbed a bandana from his back pocket to wipe up the mess.

"I can walk from here," she offered, "but I didn't get paid yet."

He took out his wallet and handed her some money. Dabbing at his crotch with his other hand, he said, "Go on, I'll see you later."

Brona was pacing the house when she opened the door, so Sarah waved the money in the air, saying, "Look! He was drunk, and accidentally gave me a fifty-dollar bill. Can I go to the mall this weekend?"

Brona held out her hand. "Not when we have bills to pay."

Sarah lifted her chin. "It's my money. Believe me, I earned it tonight."

Brona pointed to the main bedroom where Kevin was sleeping. "Do you want him to kill me when we can't pay for the power? Is that what you want?"

"Get your own job then."

Brona slapped her face, and Sarah jerked awake. Rueben was on his back snoring softly, and she laid her head on his chest, but after a minute or two, he turned over and put his back to her, so she reached for her phone on the nightstand.


Laura leaned on her kitchen counter, reliving her argument with Brian. She hadn't thought she treated him like a child, but maybe he was right. She worried about him more than she worried about Audi, and she expected less of him. He didn't understand the burden that came with their powers, thank God.

Still, it wasn't fair to either of the kids and she would have to do better. Her sister's presence floated through her mind, and she picked up her phone waiting for the ring.

When she answered, Sarah blurted, "I'm not okay. Are you okay?"

"I'm eating half a jar of peanut butter off a rice cake at two in the morning so..."

"We're in trouble, real trouble." Sarah's voice was shaking. "It's not perverts and petty criminals anymore, Lolly. What are we doing?"

She hadn't called her Lolly in years. The memories they'd tried to bury for so long were instead getting fresher and Sarah was reverting more and more to her childhood references.

Sarah liked to think that she was the mature one, the one who had it all together, and Laura had to admit that was usually true. When they were young though, Laura was the adult for the whole family and Sarah's protector. She, too, was reverting to her old ways.

"I've been working on a spell, but it needs some oomph. Can you talk to Rhonda tomorrow about getting some help from the Other Side? I'll check in with Drew and see if he's learned anything new."

Sarah let her breath out in a whoosh. "Wow. I don't believe you could've come up with a worse idea."

## Chapter Eleven

The next morning, Laura sat across from Drew at Racine's Diner stirring honey into her tea. "You know, we're supposed to be abominations," she thought out loud, "So, maybe we *are* being punished."

His heart ached for her. "Dead or alive, your mother can't deal out judgement like that."

"Are you sure? Because she nearly killed me on the way home from Flagstaff yesterday."

He rubbed the bridge of his nose. "It sounds like the attacks are getting worse as your emotions intensify."

She nodded. "I'll have to re-cover the back seat from the fireball I pitched at her. Good thing there were no highway patrol in the area."

He shuddered. The road down the mountains from Flagstaff was fairly treacherous on a day with no demons. If a passing semitruck didn't kill you, there was still the risk of plunging over the side into a canyon. Countless black skid marks on broken guardrails were a somber reminder that it had happened before. She must have been terrified, but clearly, she was able to keep her head if she'd tried to kill it with fire.

"Can we...can we talk about your powers?"

She nodded patiently, having expected that question from him for a while.

"Do you know how it works? In your body?"

"I can't create fire from inside of me, if that's what you mean. I can only manipulate it. It does what I want it to do, what I need it to do, I guess."

"You can talk to it?"

"No, it's more subconscious." A man walking by the window outside stopped to light a cigarette.

"If I really wanted to, let's say this guy was a threat of some kind, I could send that flame up his nose." She made the flame a bit higher, and the man backed his head away from the lighter.

"The element responds to your intention." He paused for a moment, both amazed and alarmed, before asking, "What if you're not sure?"

"I have to be sure."

"That's a lot of pressure."

She pursed her lips. "I guess Bash was right. I'm dangerous, probably reckless even." She felt a bit guilty as the man outside inspected his lighter for flaws. "I never thought about my life in those terms until he said it." She sipped her tea. "But I didn't think he would just walk away from me because of it."

"Anyway," she continued, "we figured it out when we were teenagers. My guess is that puberty brings that kind of thing on if it's already inside of you. As we got older, we got stronger and more exacting. Rhonda taught us to embrace it like a gift, even when Mom said it meant we would be rejected by—"

He frowned and finished her sentence, "By God."

"I didn't sell my soul," she protested. "I literally woke up like this one day and now I'm supposed to be damned? If I don't get a vote, then I don't care who's in charge. I'm just living my life."

He reached across the table and took her hand. "Hey, I'm on your side. Your response to everything makes a lot of sense. It's interesting to me that Sarah ended up gravitating toward the church instead of away from it.

"She gravitated toward you."

He choked a little on his coffee and a corner of her mouth turned up slyly.

"I'm talking about the safe space you created," she said, "and the good you do for this town. Could any other preacher sit here in broad daylight, having breakfast with a witch?" She looked around the diner. "No one is giving you so much as a side eye."

He suspected that had more to do with fear of Laura than respect for him, but kept it to himself, saying, "You know I have plenty of haters."


Outside, Bash was reliving his interview with Bob Mercer as he and Chuck crossed the street toward the diner. "I'm telling you, something's not right about the way he was acting. It was like he was waiting—getting ready."

"Tucson confirmed his story about Connie and Jenny, so we have to find out what that something is."

"I hope those women stay in Tucson for a long time."

Bash spotted Laura and Drew at a table by the window and paused with his hand on the door.

"Seat yourselves guys," the harried hostess hollered out from behind the counter.

Laura was wearing jeans and a form fitting tank top with a light, loose weave sweater over it. Her legs were crossed, and she casually flipped flopped her sandal with her toes as they talked.

Bash felt his stomach turn. "They're at breakfast?"

Chuck furrowed his brow. "Dude, she's being haunted by her mother, stalked by some prick with a big ass dog, and nursing a broken heart. Her life is a disaster right now, and he's—"

"Don't say it."

Chuck's tone softened. "Hey, you quit that job, remember?"

"I'm not hungry."

"So, we gotta go to Phoenix for coffee now? Come on, I'm buying today."

The men nodded civilly to one another as the deputies passed her table, but Laura looked out the window. Bash noticed that on her wrist was the tiger's eye bracelet he bought for her in Sedona. She'd kissed him so sweetly in the middle of that shop, but as he stood there watching Drew give her hand a supportive squeeze, the memory felt like a punch in the gut.

Bash had seen the preacher in action many times and believed Drew to be the better man of the two of them. However, he did not believe that Drew was right for her. He cursed himself, frustrated by the self-inflicted nature of all his pain.

It was no longer just a matter of getting her back, which would be no easy task, especially since it was taking him so long to figure things out, and if she was moving on it would be much more complicated.

Drew had been braced for a confrontation of some sort between the ex-lovers, but all he saw in Bash's face was regret. When the deputies found their table, he leaned close to Laura.

"He knows he made a mistake."

Her eyes flashed so dangerously that Drew scooted back in his chair.

She said, "You know, everyone keeps telling me that but him."


While they waited for their order, Chuck caught Bash stealing a glance at the table by the window."

"Look, they're not sleeping together."

"How would you know?"

"If they were, Mena would know and unfortunately, so would I."

Bash wrinkled his forehead and stared into his coffee cup. "She tells you everything?"

The waitress brought their order, and Chuck dug into his eggs.

"Did they talk about..." Bash pointed to himself.

"I know more about your dick," Chuck said, taking a bite and pointing his empty fork at Bash, "honestly, more than I'm comfortable with, man."

Bash threw his head back and laughed. "Well, she's so pissed at me, you'll probably never have to hear about it again."

Chuck crunched on a piece of bacon and said, "Seriously though, for what it's worth, I also heard that you could fix this if you really want to."

Drew held the door as they left the restaurant. "I don't believe you're damned, but this demon is part of you and its either got to be reabsorbed or banished somehow before it kills you both."

She dug her keys out of her purse, "I don't love the idea of absorbing it and I've been working on a cord cutting spell of sorts. The logistics are complicated though—we're getting some help from the Other Side."

He squeezed his eyes closed in exasperation, so she touched him reassuringly. "It's just an insurance policy, Drew."

"Have you got any idea what the premium will be?"

A shadow crossed her face, but then she grinned and said, "It can't be any more than I paid when Brian started driving."

"I'm going with you."

She kissed him on the cheek. "I guess you're a part of the family now." She waved and started off across the street.

*Part of the family.* Both his occupation and his calling dictated that he stayed just outside the realm of most personal involvement. Even so, he was proud to be someone gifted at leading others out of darkness. As he aged though, he found himself hungry for the intimacy and belonging that his work cost him. His soul was weary from plodding through his own darkness and Laura had no idea how she'd just fed his heart.

He started for the parking lot, running straight into the man from the bar. His dog sat nearby on the curb.

The man ran his hand slowly up and down Drew's back. "You're quite brave, Andrew. Are you sure God will forgive this alliance?"

Drew squirmed and his stomach rolled. "Leave us alone."

The dog barked a warning, and the two sprinted across the street, leaving Drew doubling over into Chuck's arms as the as the deputies ran out of the diner. Chuck gathered him up and leaned him against the wall.

"Was that the guy? The one the women took down at Isaac's?" Chuck lifted Drew's head and gave his face a light smack. "He made you sick, didn't he? Bash, the guy is like poison. You should have seen it."

Bash clenched his fists and scanned the street. "Yeah, I should have."

"Laura," Drew gasped, and Bash sprinted off in the direction the preacher pointed.

She spun around, keys buried in between her fingers, when she heard him jog up behind her. He could see no one else was around, so he slowed and did his best to keep his voice calm.

"Hey."

Her breath caught in her throat, but she projected as much righteous indignation as she could muster while avoiding his eyes.

He looked around again for the man and his dog but saw no one. Apparently, she was safe, so he decided it was as good a time as any to talk.

"Listen, I'm sorry about the tracker."

She crossed her arms and studied the sky, still refusing to look at him.

"I know it was wrong, I just," he caught himself making excuses and stopped. "That's it. I'm sorry."

"You can't have it both ways, Bash. You're either in, or you're out."

"What if I told you I'm trying to figure out a way to deal with..."

"Ugh," she sighed in frustration, "why are you working so hard to fit us both into boxes we don't belong in?"

It was his turn to look away, unable to come up with an answer good enough for either of them.

She unlocked the Jeep, and as he reached around her to open the door, she didn't pull away when his fingers grazed hers, but she kept her back to him, and climbed in.

When he shut the door, she finally met his gaze. "Apology accepted."

She leaned her head on the seat back and watched him walk away, whispering to herself, "Jesus give me strength."

The man and his dog stood watching from a few cars down. "Jesus doesn't care about you, sweetheart."

## Chapter Twelve

"The Other Side? You of all people know better than that." Rhonda handed Sarah and Audi glasses of iced tea and wiped her forehead with a napkin. "Can you believe this heat already?" They were sitting on Rhonda's back porch, enjoying her view of the mountains.

"Laura's spell isn't strong enough; she's already tried it."

Rhonda frowned. "So, work on it."

Audi stretched her long legs in front of her on the porch swing. "We're running out of time, and we don't know what's up with dog man."

Rhonda was doubtful. "There's been so much activity from that realm lately, and do you know what? I ran into Sebastian at Arley's the other day when I was getting gas. There's even been a murder in this town. He thinks it's all connected.

Sarah raised an eyebrow. "He just *told* you that? Out of the blue?"

"Oh, I got onto him for giving up on Laura. That man knows damn well he's not getting any younger, and that those two ought to be treating each other like gold instead of being so stubborn." She set her glass down and waved her finger in the air. "I know what his problem is. He thinks he wants his witch to sell her tea and spend her days worrying about him while he's out there fighting bad guys. But that's not what really turns him on. Hell, didn't they fight goblins together the night they met?"

She took another napkin from the tray and wiped the condensation from her glass. "Anyway, I think he got nervous and changed the subject. He asked me if I'd seen anything strange at Mercer's place, you know, because that family's just down the road from here."

Sarah exchanged an amused glance with her daughter. She would have given a lot of money to see that conversation go down.

Rhonda looked over her eyeglasses at Sarah. "It doesn't do to spend your last years of life being miserable. Anyway, back to the point, you'll have to stay alert out there." She fanned her face with her napkin. "And you've got to make friends, so what's your gift?"

Audi took a plastic grocery bag out of her satchel and stood by the lemon tree. "May I?"

Rhonda nodded but kept her eyes on Sarah. "Where will you start?"

"I'm afraid we have to find that stupid rabbit."


"This is really what they want?" Drew wondered aloud as he stood at the counter slicing lemons. "Not a piece of your soul, or your child, or…?"

"Hey!" Audi protested.

Laura's kitchen was cheery, with sunshine-colored walls and greenery spilling over the top of every cabinet, and she sat with one leg tucked underneath her at the breakfast nook by the window. He imagined she spent countless hours leaning against the frayed pillows with a cup of tea and a book.

She stripped tiny leaves from a sprig of thyme and regarded him patiently. "They don't have much use for us, let alone our souls."

The beings they sought out had so little use for humans that Laura knew they were risking their lives just trying to find them. Simplicity was key, and she'd decided on that particular offering because certain things in the magical realm were universal, no matter what Side you lived on. Her greeting potion included lemon juice for friendship, thyme for health and courage, lavender to keep things calm and honey to sweeten the deal. She hoped their intentions would be clear enough.

Sarah handed him a bowl for the lemons and met his eyes with a warning. "Don't underestimate them and don't let your guard down. Their society functions on ideals that will seem foreign to us, and they're unpredictable at best." Then she gave him a wink and a playful nudge. "But they'll love this, and it's even better if you add vodka."

Their inhibitions had fallen away once he was accepted into their world, and he was not surprised to learn that he adored them even more. It was hard for him not to judge Rueben and Sebastian for their absence, but he was pretty sure they were the ones suffering the most for their actions.

"Excellent idea, Mom, let's pregame the suicide mission." She dipped her finger in the honey. "I guess if they do kill us, we're done worrying about all of this and the problem is solved."

Drew looked up from his thoughts. "That's a pretty big problem for me."

Laura half-filled an enormous jar with water and set it next to the other ingredients. "Bury your negativity," she instructed. "They'll be able to sense it and our intention is to show goodwill." Sarah and Audi gathered around the jar, then they all looked at Drew.

He recoiled a bit and said, "I don't have any powers."

Sarah blinked at him. "Do you have thoughts?"

He nodded stupidly.

"Then, make them happy and put them in the jar."

When they parked in front of a large rock formation covered in petroglyphs, Audi leaned over to Drew in the back seat. "If things get out of hand, we haul ass back to the car."

"We're hiking in?"

Laura slung the backpack over her shoulder and said, "We would even if it wasn't far because they can't tolerate iron.

He dug in his pocket and pulled out his knife, then reached behind him for his gun. Everyone in Chuparosa was armed, and Andrew carried a Smith and Wesson MP Shield 9mm. It was small enough to conceal, but powerful enough to put down anything from a rattlesnake to a robber. He handed them up to Sarah, who put them in the center console.

"No weapons, no sudden movements. They'll be suspicious of everything we do."

"We're really putting ourselves in their hands," he grumbled, "this is a terrible idea."

"Yeah, it is." Laura agreed. "Sarah will lead the way because they're drawn to her."

They walked silently, single file, along the canyon ridge for about a mile-and-a-half when they came across an owl sitting on a Barrel cactus. When Sarah stepped around, it spread its wings and flapped wildly at them.

"I guess we're not going that way," Audi murmured.

Before they could decide on a new direction, the jackrabbit with towering red ears popped out from behind the cactus and stared them down.

Laura held out her arms to steady herself. "Are you dizzy?"

"Yep." Sarah turned to the others. "Here we go."

The jackrabbit started on a path down the canyon wall, a path that hadn't been there before. It hopped a few yards and turned to look at them.

Drew hesitated. "We're just supposed to follow it?"

The women didn't answer but set off down the path, leaving him to catch up. It was steep, and they had to scramble to keep pace with the rabbit who kept disappearing in the bushes.

Sarah swore. "Well, we're almost down, so let's keep going without him." She needn't have worried because the rabbit reappeared as they reached the wash at the bottom of the canyon.

Drew touched Sarah's shoulder and brought her attention to dark clouds forming to the southwest. It wasn't quite monsoon season, but the area was prone to thunderstorms and flash floods at any time, and they were deep in a canyon.

"You got a plan, pal?" he said to the rabbit.

Audi stifled a shriek and backed into her aunt. A bobcat sat atop a large boulder just ahead of them and though the rabbit's body quaked a bit at the sight of it, he held a steady course toward the rocks.

"Great." Sarah grabbed Audi's hand and pushed her behind the group even though the bobcat was no bigger than a dog. Its scruffy beard and stubby tail gave it the look of a stuffed animal, but while bobcats didn't typically attack humans, they knew it could easily kill one of them with a well-placed swipe of the claws.

"Aaaaaand there are two of them." Drew reached behind him for his gun and cursed when he remembered it was still in the car.

The second bobcat continued past them, then peered over its shoulder, so Sarah started out after it. "We follow him, too."

The bobcat led them down the wash to a shallow cave in the wall of the canyon, then it went inside and positioned itself to face them. The rabbit reappeared with the first bobcat, and they remained just outside. A fox walked past them from behind and entered the cave on the opposite side of the bobcat. Laura pointed to the ring of black fur around its front left foot.

"It's the fox from the other day."

"I told you."

In the not too far off distance, they heard a scream.

Drew's breath quickened. "Oh, my God."

A mountain lion's roar is often mistaken for a woman's scream, but through a combination of bad experiences, they all knew the difference. The other animals looked up and the humans froze in horror as the mountain lion they'd just heard crested the ridge. Her long tail swished back and forth in annoyance as she stared down at them.

Audi fainted and when Drew started for her, Sarah stopped him.

"This is better. Leave her."

The mountain lion was easily five feet long. Her ash-colored fur looked deceptively soft, as if you could bury your face in her neck for snuggles until her claws ripped you to shreds. The humans cried out and covered their ears as her voice echoed through their heads.

"You dare!"

After a moment, Laura regained her composure and took a step forward. "We mean no disrespect. I...I have a spell for your review. I want to cast out a demon, but it's not strong enough."

Every instinct was telling the others to run but they lined up alongside Laura. The mountain lion leapt from her perch and entered the cave, immediately flanked by the bobcats. The jackrabbit bounded up to her, but she glowered at it and stomped her gigantic paw down on one of its ears and ground it into the sand.

Sarah shivered. It would probably be punished later for showing them the way.

In their heads, the mountain lion spoke again. "What do you expect Adira to do?"

Drew was fascinated and couldn't help himself from asking, "Is that your name? Adira?"

The big cat ignored him and focused on the women. "This demon is your own creation, and it is splendid. Why destroy it?"

*Interesting.* Laura thought. *If she can talk in our heads, it makes sense she can read our minds, too.*

"If you know our thoughts, then you know we don't mean to hurt you."

Audi woke just then and this time Drew went to her. She shrieked and burrowed herself into his arms when she saw her mother and aunt facing the cougar at the cave entrance.

He put his mouth to her ear. "Shhh, don't say a word."

Adira motioned to the bobcats, who approached Laura and sniffed at her backpack. "What do you have for me?"

Laura slid the pack off her shoulder and the animals sank defensively into their front paws, ready to pounce.

"It's okay." She handed the gallon jug to Sarah. Then she took out the porcelain bowl and they entered the cave. Drew and Audi attempted to follow but the bobcats barred their way. Laura set the bowl on the ground in front of Adira and Sarah opened the spout to pour the lemonade. The fox stepped warily forward, looking from the women to Adira, but after a few tentative sips he began to slurp it up.

Audi grabbed Drew's arm. "He likes it!"

Adira took her foot off the rabbit's ear and dipped her own head in the bowl. In their minds they heard, "Where is your spell?"

Laura pulled the spell jar from the backpack and held it out. One of the bobcats disappeared to the back of the cave and returned with a large open geode in its jaws that it dropped at Sarah's feet. The geode sloshed with a thick, sweet-smelling liquid.

Adira pushed at it with her paw and nudged at Laura's hip with her shoulders. The strength behind that nudge very nearly knocked Laura off her feet, but she kept her focus and immersed her spell jar in the geode.

Adira scolded her as the crystal encrusted rock began to pulse with a violet luminescence. "The spell is strong, but its core lacks conviction and you knew this. You will have to commit to your work and this power fades as the sun crosses the sky."

The big cat took another drink from Laura's bowl then bounded into the rocks and out of the canyon. The bobcats and the fox went their separate ways, but the jackrabbit remained in the cave, pawing at its bloody ear.

Sarah approached it with trepidation. "Do you remember me?"

It bared long fangs and hissed at her.

"I guess you do," she whispered, and poured the rest of the lemonade in the bowl.

Drew took her arm as thunder rumbled in the distance and fat drops of rain fell on the sand.

"We have to go."

## *Chapter Thirteen*

When they reached the vehicle, Sarah looked up at the cloudy sky and then to her cellphone on the seat. "Almost noon-there's not much time."

Audi dug around in the back seat for supplies. "How are you supposed to summon it?" She asked.

Laura hung her head and kicked at the dirt. "How old were you the first time Mom called you a whore?"

The flowers on the nearest cactus withered and fell to the ground when Sarah answered, "I was eleven."

The air around them grew thick with pain as their memories flowed. Audi was used to it and had mental protections in place, but Drew was overwhelmed by emotion. His hands balled into fists as involuntary tears welled in his eyes.

Audi found the box of salt she'd been looking for and sprinkled out the beginnings of a circle around herself and Drew.

"What are you doing?" He asked.

"This is not our circus. We are strictly ornamental right now."

"Does that work?"

"Well, they swear by the technique, but you are part of my first test group, so we'll see."

From the driver's side, a tall, sinewy creature with black eyes and long talons hulked toward the sisters, making Drew anxious. "It's so much bigger now."

Audi's hands shook, and she quickly finished her circle.

Laura held the geode up and the women inched toward the demon posing as their mother.

Brona's face hardened as she examined the rock. "What do you think you're doing?"

"You're not welcome here." Laura held the spell in front of her.

It was subtle, but the demon's features began to transform. Brona's hair thinned and the bones in her cheeks sharpened. "You brought me here, and you can't just toss me aside." She sneered at the spell. "Who do you think you are?"

The sisters advanced on her, and she raised her hand, as if ready to slap one of them. "Don't make me count to three."

Laura's arms lowered slightly, but Sarah was unmoved. "We said you're not welcome here." The sun emerged from behind the clouds, and she noted the time. "Laura, focus."

Brona lowered her hand and met Laura's eyes. "You know I did my best. I was afraid of you little monsters. Can you really blame me for that?"

"Lolly, do it."

Brona threw herself on to her belly in front of them. It was trick they'd seen it before—she was not above throwing a literal tantrum to manipulate them. "At least you'll get what you always wanted, and as a bonus, you'll get to kill me yourself. That should make you feel better. Won't it make you feel better?"

Laura tried to imagine what it would have been like if Brian had been born with powers she didn't understand. She would never have been cruel to him, but wouldn't she have been afraid? "I didn't want you to die, Mom."

It's not your mother, Laura." Drew reached for her, but Audi held him in the circle.

"Come on, Auntie," She whispered.

Brona began to sob. "You broke my heart with your wicked ways, and I only did what I thought was right."

Lightning crackled behind the demon, and as thunder rocked the canyon, Laura hurled the geode at the rocks behind her. Shards flew as it exploded, and flames outlined the petroglyphs.

Sarah grabbed her by the shoulders. "What did you do?"

Adira's roar echoed through the desert around them. Laura and Sarah backed against the rocks, and Drew ran to the Cherokee for his gun. From behind, arms wrapped around his chest and pulled him backward. His body convulsed and he struggled to breathe as the scent of evil filled his lungs.

He felt the man's breath on his neck. "You should have stayed in your little circle."

Audi started to run for Drew, but the dog appeared before her, growling.

Brona sat up and scooted backward to lean against a tire, grinning and twisting her hair with her fingers.

Adira jumped down from the rocks and Audi screamed, "Look out!"

The mountain lion swiped down at the women, and they dove away grabbing their ears as Adira's voice rang in their heads. "Weak!" She screamed and leapt down, pushing a giant paw into Laura's chest.

"Please don't!" Laura cried.

Drew struggled as the man dragged him to the circle and dropped him, gasping for breath, next to the dog.

The man raised his hand to stop Adira, but she shook her head in defiance, lowering her face to Laura's while raising her other front paw in the air and extending her claws. The dog barked and Laura screamed, and Audi cried and through the chaos, they heard the man's low and icy voice say, "Do not hurt her."

Laura looked in confusion from Adira to the man from the bar. Adira flattened her ears and used a claw to pick at the shattered geode.

"This insult will not go unanswered." Adira said, and Laura screamed in pain as she dragged her claws across her belly.

The man approached Adira and ran his hand along her back. "Let her go. Now."

She shook him off but did as she was told, releasing her hold on Laura as Sarah crawled to her sister and pressed a hand to her bleeding abdomen.

Adira put her face nose to nose with the man and let out another roar before leaping into the rocks and disappearing across the desert.

The man knelt beside Laura and examined her wounds. Even though her blood oozed freely, Adira had used remarkable restraint, so the slashes weren't very deep. His touch sent a pulse of energy through Laura's body.

"Correct me if I'm wrong," he smirked, "but I just witnessed what humans call an epic fail, did I not?"

Laura grasped his hand. "Did you put that demon on us?"

"Oh no, my sweet babies, you did that all by yourselves." Sarah moved his hand away from Laura's body but still he beamed at them. "It's impressive. I had hoped my girls would go into STEM-I'm progressive that way-but you're so creative. Who would have thought you would come up with your very own demon?"

He gestured at Drew. "I'd rather see you with a better class of friends, but that's on me. I admit I wasn't around enough during your formative years."

Sarah stood and went for the first aid kit in the Cherokee. "Who are you?"

"You can call me Daddy."

She glared at him. "I don't think so."

"Oh alright, fair enough. At some point, you will have to face the facts, but I've also been known to go by Thomas."

"What do you want?"

While Sarah tended Laura's wounds, he traced the petroglyphs with his fingers as he launched into his story.

"A long time ago there was a race of half-angels almost like you. We tried to improve on the original recipe when we made them. Humans back then were fragile, confused little sheep, and babysitting them was torture. Honestly, we were only trying to help. Our first babies were big and clumsy, the proverbial bulls in a China shop. They broke everything, and we...we got in big, big trouble." He rubbed at deep ugly scars on his wrists.

Laura sat up on her elbows. "What did you do to our mother?"

"We made a deal."

"Oh, my God." She laid back down when the realization hit.

He put his hand under her shoulder and again waves of energy ran through her body as he stood her on her feet and reached for Sarah. When she recoiled, he jerked her up by the arm and the same force flowed through her.

"I'd long ago abandoned you as another failed experiment, but when I learned Brona was dying, I thought I'd check in one last time, just to make sure."

Sarah shuddered. "You set the goblins loose…and the revenant."

He clapped his hands excitedly, "Which you completely destroyed. Well done, by the way. I dislike goblins intensely. You're so interesting. I mean, I guess I should have known you would be." He smacked his forehead. "Women are, of course."

Laura cringed. "What do you want from us?"

"What I wanted all along. To join forces, to do better than was done before."

The dog guarded Audi closely, so Drew quietly made his way to the gun that had fallen by the vehicle.

He stood and pointed it at Thomas. "Get away from them!"

Without looking his way, Thomas grabbed Drew's hand and again the gun fell. He pushed Drew down and continued. "I want to make up for prior mistakes," he waved his hand dismissively, "inconsistencies, really. In the end, my children will help me build my home."

"Isn't Hell your home?" Drew choked.

Thomas kicked him in the ribs.

"Stop!" Laura shrieked.

Sarah fell to her knees next to Drew and said, "We are not doing shit for you."

"Like I didn't know you would say that. Again, it's my bad, you were not raised properly. This has just been an introductory visit, so we'll talk more soon."

He snapped his fingers at the dog. "Get some rest, darlings."

"Well, that sucked." Audi put whiskey shots on the table in front of Laura, Sarah, and Drew. They were back in Laura's kitchen ignoring a couple of pizzas they'd picked up on the way. No one seemed hungry for anything except the shots.

Drew sat down, carefully holding his ribs and started to say, "Obviously we misjudged—"

Sarah put her finger up to stop him, then turned on her sister and exploded. "What were you thinking? That was our one chance. You always let her get to you. You're an emotional disaster."

Laura had been waiting for that. Her eyes flashed at Sarah, but she kept her tone measured. "At least I have emotions."

Audi helped Drew to stand and led him across the room where she retrieved an ice pack from the freezer and lifted his t-shirt.

Sarah paced in front of her sister. "So what? I'm a robot because I'm not prone to freaking out the way you do? I didn't let Mom's hatefulness define me. I didn't go crazy and skip college or end up a single mother."

"No, you did everything right. You settled for the first man who came along and tucked yourself into a well-ordered life. You used him as your excuse not to deal with her and let his coldness seep all the way through you."

"That's not fair!"

"Why didn't you work the spell then?" Laura challenged.

"You know you're better at spells than I am."

"Why?"

"What do you want from me?"

"Spells are desires and feelings and intentions. You remember those things, right?"

"Don't turn this around." Sarah pointed her finger. "You fucked up today. It would have been so easy, especially since we got help—"

Laura cut her off. "Help from the Other Side? Those inhuman creatures who don't give a damn about us? Those beings who can't feel? Did you ever wonder why you relate to them so much?"

"I swear to God, Laura, if you don't stop…"

Drew opened his mouth to intervene, but before he got the chance, Sarah's phone vibrated, and the default ring tone sliced through the tension in the room.

"Steve called out tonight, so I'm on my way to the station," Reuben said when she answered.

Sarah rubbed her temples. "Why do *you* have to go?"

"Dammit, Sarah, who else is gonna do it? I'll just check the place out and take care of a few other things while I'm there. I think the Sheriff's still working, so there's probably not much happening. Where have you been all day anyway?"

She snapped, "What do you care?" and hung up.

Audi put Drew's ice to her forehead. "Welcome to the family."

He lowered his head and snuck off to the bathroom. Examining the bruises Thomas left behind, he supposed that he was lucky to be alive. In fact, they all were. He would never recover from watching Adira slice through Laura's belly. Things might have been different if she had completed the spell, but there was no way to know. Leaning against the door, he closed his eyes, whispering, "Everything is coming apart-why won't you help us?"

"Wait." Laura gave a short laugh. "You don't even have a special ringtone for your husband?"

Sarah sniffed. "Your ringtone for Brian's dad is the Imperial March. What do you have for Sebastian? Radioactive?"

Audi snorted.

Laura began to shake with sobs, and Sarah handed her a dish towel. "Look, neither one of us is wrong and it even looks like Mom was right, too. We *are* abominations, literal Hell spawn, apparently. So many things are starting to make sense now."

"I don't believe that, and neither should you," Drew said as he left the bathroom. Snatching his  ice from Audi, he added, "We don't know what's really happening or if he's even telling the truth. What I do know is that you two are invaluable to this town, to each other, and to me. Thomas apparently needs you for whatever he's planning too, so we have to figure out how to stop him. I suggest you knock this shit off and think about reclaiming the power you gave to that demon because you're going to need it back. All of it." He opened the back door. "If we live through the night, I'll see you tomorrow, and we'll figure this out together."

When he was gone, Laura wiped the dish towel across her eyes. "We've upset our new big brother."

Sarah took Audi by the hand and headed for the open door. "He's right. We'll talk about this tomorrow."

They needed rain in the area desperately, but the storm remained mostly wind and dust. The kitchen lights flickered with the lightning outside, and Laura's head began to swim.

There was a burning sensation where Adira's claws had raked across her skin and she examined her bloody, shredded t-shirt wondering which potion she might deploy. If there had been a bit more pressure behind that paw, she would be the emergency room's problem, or more likely, the morgue's.

Was the lion's claw poisonous or would the wound simply be ugly and painful? She'd had some success with yarrow, but maybe a simple mugwort poultice would work. In the end she just didn't trust herself enough that night and settled on Bactine.

Having raised an adventurous son, she kept first aid in almost every room of the house. A cool breeze floated across the back of her neck as she fetched the kit from the pantry and she was not surprised when she turned to see her mother at the table, leaning on her elbows.

"I bet you never saw any of this coming," the Brona demon said.

Laura's eyes darted around the room. Every door and window had been protected, so how was she getting into their homes? At that moment, she was too tired to feel, and for the first time, she examined the creature with no emotional association. She noted the sharpness of the features, the length of the nose, and the subtle pointedness of the ears. Brona was a lovely woman with soft curves and a round face. Her skin remained smooth until the end, but the face of the thing in front of Laura was angular and riddled with deep lines.

How had she not noticed that before? She'd been so desperate to believe her mother's ghost was reaching out, somehow providing closure, but though it responded to their emotions, it rarely spoke to them directly. Perhaps they'd been putting words in its mouth the whole time, giving it the same power that they'd given their mother when she was alive.

She'd been humoring Andrew up to that point but as his wisdom finally sank in, she couldn't believe her foolishness. Their wards weren't working because they were carrying the thing inside of them everywhere they went.

She glared at Brona's impersonator. "I am not doing this with you right now."

She decided to physically drag it out of her house and lunged across the table, but the demon squealed and squeezed itself into a corner.

Laura found she was too tired to fight it anyway so she closed her eyes and shouted, "Get out of my house!"

It didn't take long for the air to shift, and she was alone when she opened her eyes. She picked up her phone and moved to press Sarah's number but stopped herself and scrolled through the rest of her 'favorites.' Andrew had been through enough for one day. The poor man was in a full-blown crisis of faith because of them.

She looked at the time. Mena would be busy getting her family fed. Finally, she let her thumb hover over his name. Bash's ringtone was, in fact, the beginning of Wicked Game, by Chris Isaak. Sarah would vomit.

She put the phone down and smiled sadly. In crisis situations, normal women usually called their mothers.

## Chapter Fourteen

Wind whipped around Thomas as he loitered outside watching the two men working in the station. He didn't care about the brown skinned one-it was just that guy's bad luck that they were always together. Laura cared way too much about the cowboy though, and it was time to put her priorities in order.

Bash hovered over the surveillance photos of Bob Mercer that were strewn out on his desk as Chuck picked one up, studied it for a minute and flicked it back.

"What's with this guy? He's been acting like a madman ever since you two killed that zombie."

"Revenant," Bash corrected. "Look at his eyes, I don't even think that's Bob anymore."

"What? Do you think we have a new creature on our hands?" Chuck sat down. "We've got to talk to the Deanes about this. I think there's a lot more going on and we're way out of the loop."

Bash swallowed. "Fine. I'll go see Laura tomorrow."

"So she can throw something heavier at your head this time? I don't think so. I'll go."

Bash didn't respond to that. Instead, he looked out the window and noted that the wind was picking up. "We're gonna get some weather tonight."

"Nah, just dust."

The lights flickered and the door shook violently, so Bash took a flashlight out of the drawer and set it on the desk. A handful of rain drops swirled through the air with the dust to create a thin film of mud on everything outside. "Crap, I just washed my truck,"

He stood and stretched his arms overhead. One of his legs was asleep from sitting for too long, so he limped toward the door for a closer look at the storm. He was halfway across the room when it swung open, wind blowing pictures and papers all over the room.

"Wasn't that locked?"

Chuck didn't answer, he stared past Bash at the man strolling through the door and he recognized him right away.

Thomas was wearing black jeans, black boots, a white t-shirt and a black denim jacket. His dark hair whipped around his shoulders with the wind.

"This building is closed." Chuck said calmly but without blinking. "Can we help you with something?"

"Possibly," Thomas drawled, "I need to get the attention of a Miss Laura Deane."

Bash narrowed his eyes. "What do you want with her?"

"Well son, I'm her father."

Bash drew his gun. "Bullshit."

Chuck touched Bash's arm and said, "Easy, friend," then refocused on Thomas. "What are you playing at, man?"

Thomas picked a photo off the floor. "Poor Bob doesn't know what to do with himself right now, but I'll have an assignment for him soon."

Bash stepped forward with his gun still trained on the intruder. "Who are you? How are you pulling Mercer's strings?"

Thomas took off his jacket and laid it across the guest chair in front of Bash's desk, then let a pair of wings the color of smoke unfurl behind him.

Chuck drew his own gun. "What the hell?"

"You are correct, sir." Thomas' hands began to crackle with thin blue strands of electricity. "My baby girl just needs a little motivation right now. I considered going right for her boy but you're closer."

Chuck threw Bash a look. "Oh, no-Brian."

Bash cocked his pistol. "Where is Brian?"

Thomas looked at his watch. "In his dorm, I'm guessing. Or maybe he's banging..." he put a finger to his chin, "Olivia, I believe is her name. She's a physics major. Anyway, at this moment in time he fascinates me, so I'm hoping that you," he nodded at Bash, "are the one who will help me convince Laura to cooperate."

"Why would I do that? Cooperate on what?"

"Hmm," Thomas peered at Bash for a long moment. "It's not just your body that aches for her, is it?"

Bash took another step forward. "Be careful what you say next."

Thomas clapped his hands and spun in a circle. "Have I stumbled into a Lifetime Movie of the Week?"

He met Bash in the center of the room. "Are you really that worried about losing her in some magical monster battle, or are you just chapped because you can't control her actions?" He shook his head in disgust. "That peace you found in her arms? That kind of soul level happiness is reserved for a precious few, and you're an idiot to let it go."

Bash pushed his gun into Thomas' chest and flicked at the silver tip on his wing. "I don't care who you are. I'm not doing shit for you."

"I didn't come here to give you a script to read to her. Your role is much more passive." He extended his arm and a beam of electricity surged from his hand into an outlet behind the desk sending a thin line of fire up the wall.

Chuck ran to the other side of the room and pulled the fire alarm.

Thomas laughed. "One of the things I love about small towns in the middle of nowhere is the lengthy emergency response time."

He faced Bash again. "How does it feel to know that you'll never be able to make it right? I'll bet that preacher does his best to comfort her when you're gone."

Bash pulled the trigger. Thomas gave his body an astonishingly quick twitch to the left and the bullet passed him, hitting the wall across the room. The deputies backed away as the angel formed a fireball between his hands.

The whites of his eyes expanded until the entire sockets glowed. "I doubt it will get you any special treatment, but when you fellas get to Hell, tell them Thomas sent you." He wound up his arm, then Chuck and Bash dove in opposite directions as the fireball exploded between them.

Daniel watched at the window while Thomas toyed with the men inside. He could not predict exactly how Laura would respond to Sebastian's death, but he knew that Thomas was wrong.

There was no scenario in which she would bestow her loyalty on the one who murdered the man she loved. If anything, she would focus all of her efforts against him, complicating Daniel's work, and she would no doubt set his progress back by centuries.

He was currently tasked with either adding the Deane sisters to his list of Defenses or stopping them outright. He preferred the former, and while Sebastian was no innocent, he would make a fine addition to the team and Daniel needed him alive in order to make any of it happen. No matter what, he would not let those men die so soon before their time.

Thomas disappeared, and Daniel spread his wings between the deputies and the flaming debris as the building erupted. Seeing them relatively safe, he raised his arms and muttered in the language of his kind to calm the fires.

Rueben could see the smoke and flames from down the street and sped up. "Jesus!"

He jumped from his truck and pulled out his phone. The flames had died down, but the entire front of the building was reduced to rubble. As he shouted his location at the 911 operator, he saw someone moving amongst the debris inside. "Oh, my God."

He stepped over the rubble to where Bash was hauling himself to his feet and pointing to the back of what was once the room. "Chuck is hurt."

They dragged Chuck away from the debris and later, Bash held his friend's broken arm steady while the paramedics applied a splint. In addition to the arm, they were both covered in lacerations and burns, but otherwise okay.

"We should be dead," Chuck wheezed.

Bash flicked a piece of cement out of his collar, "Just hold still."

Rueben called Sarah and Sarah called Mena, who was just then screeching up to the building in her Corolla. Firefighters put out the last of the flames, and since Rueben assumed a gas leak was to blame, a crew from Chuparosa Utilities was on the scene rolling out yellow caution tape to secure the area.

A young paramedic named Noah took Bash by the arm and led him to sit on a decorative rock outside the building. Bash tried to shake him off, but Noah was nimble and strong, and Bash was tired and hurt.

"Sheriff, look at me please." He picked a few pieces of glass out of the cut over Bash's eye and dabbed at it with a cotton pad.

"You need stitches, you've been burned, and you're in shock. Come on, take a ride with us."

Bash shook his head. "I'm not leaving, kid, look around. Can't you just..." He made a sewing motion with his fingers.

Noah's lips formed a thin line, and he looked his stubborn patient up and down. He'd worked on enough cops to know that he would not win the argument. With a sigh, he laid his hand on Bash's shoulder and said, "Wait here."

Soon, Noah returned with a small suture kit and informed Bash, "This is going to hurt."

"Just do it."

It did hurt-a lot. Bash glared at the kid and gingerly touched the bandage over his eye while Noah moved to attend to the burns on his neck.

Rueben headed their way and after barking orders into his phone, he parked himself on the rock beside Bash. "How in the hell did you guys survive that?"

Noah finished his work and grabbed a clipboard off the top of his duffel. "Sheriff, you need to sign this form."

"What?"

"You are refusing further medical treatment."

Bash signed and waved him away, then called after him, "Hey, thanks."

As Noah left, the night crew supervisor from the utility company approached them. The patch on his shirt read "Adam". Both Rueben and Bash frequently worked late into the night and had seen him around, but no one knew him very well.

Rueben stood and started quizzing him. "Shouldn't you be evacuating everyone?"

"There's no gas leak here," Adam announced. He put his hands on his hips and stared at the building for a long moment before casting a suspicious eye on the other two men. "It might not have been anything other than faulty wiring," focusing on Sebastian, he added, "You should let me know soon how deep I need to go on this."

Bash gave his appreciation for Adam's discretion and when the supervisor was out of earshot, turned to Rueben. "Laura and Sarah are in the middle of something that's gotten way out of hand. How much do you know about what they've been up to?"


Bash lived in a cozy three-bedroom Santa Fe style house on Alta Vista Road. It was the only Santa Fe on that street and one of only two houses for sale when he moved to town.

The other house was a ranch style on a half-acre corner lot, and though it was much too big for a single man, his realtor was emphatic that he at least take a look. The more he learned about Chuparosa, the more he figured that ranch house was probably haunted as hell, and the realtor was desperate to get rid of it.

Fortunately, he'd taken one look at the wooden beams and kiva fireplace and made an offer on Alta Vista without ever viewing the ranch. He wouldn't be able to explain it if you asked him, but in forty-nine years, it was the first place that ever felt like home.

He slammed the door, tossed his keys in the bowl, and left a trail of torn, bloody clothes all the way to the bathroom. With his head against the shower wall, he let the hot water pelt his back until steam filled the stall, then he swiped the cedarwood soap Laura gave him out of the dish and began to scrub. When at last the suds circled the drain clear of blood and dirt, he wrapped a towel around his waist and stood in front of the mirror.

Rueben and Chuck were right, he shouldn't be alive. Thomas had essentially thrown a bomb at them, but the fire went out almost as quickly as it started. He and

Chuck literally walked away from it and the building didn't sustain too much damage. He mentally filed that with 'future Bash's problems' and shifted his focus to things within his control at that moment.

Wincing, he pulled the bandage from over his eye and dug around in a drawer for more gauze and tape. The kid had done a good job, but Laura would have something to help it heal faster.

*Christ…Laura.* It was infuriating, but Thomas was right. He was pissing away happiness because it didn't look like it was supposed to. Laura didn't want someone to take care of her. She wanted a partner; someone she could combine forces with whether they were fighting monsters or doing the dishes. His badge sat by the sink, taunting him with the irony. If he knew anything, it was how to be a good partner, so why was he making it so hard?

He dabbed on some antibiotic ointment and reflected a bit on his life. It was too painful an exercise to conduct on a regular basis, but right then he forced himself to consider just a few of the things that made him shudder with regret: the men he'd killed, the wasteful death of his wife, the women he'd left behind in her wake, and the child he barely knew.

That he was marked for death by an angel from Hell didn't surprise him too much. That the angel was the father of the love of his life was a plot twist he'd never be able to wrap his brain around.

It was getting late, so he picked up his phone but then thought better of it. He would go to her, he would say his piece, and she would either slam the door in his face or fuck his brains out. Knowing her there would be no in-between. Even if he'd been replaced, he would be damned before he let Thomas hurt them. Laura, Drew, and the rest of that family would need help, so he would suck it up and be there for them.

## Chapter Fifteen

Sarah called Laura to tell her about the fire at the Sheriff's station and that as far as she knew, everyone was okay. Laura had just hung up when the doorbell rang. She was wearing only a pair of pajama shorts and a tank top with the bottom of the shirt tucked under her breasts because her wounds were still a little wet with Bactine. Unwilling to put up with any more bullshit, she pulled the flame from a candle into her palm and jerked open the door.

Bash put his hands up and said, "It's just me."

He was wearing faded jeans, a soft gray t-shirt with a black and gray plaid button down over it. Fear gripped her heart at the sight of tiny drops of blood peeking through a bandage over his eye. She lowered the flame and tossed it on the ground where he stomped it out for her.

He gathered that they'd shared a similarly crappy day, and she had the look of someone who *wished a mother fucker would.*

Still, her voice shook, belying her *don't test me* scowl. "Are you okay, Sebastian?"

He didn't answer but gaped at the slashes across her midsection. "Are *you* okay?"

She pulled her top down and ushered him in. "We pissed off the Other Side, I mean *really* pissed them off. But I'll be fine. Sarah and Audi are fine. Drew is fine."

His jaw tightened. "That preacher was there? He was with you when this happened?" He ran a hand through his hair. "God dammit."

Her cheeks flushed with fury. "He was helping us- what is your problem? Why are you even here?"

Less than five minutes and things had already gone sideways, so he took a deep breath and started over, saying simply, "Laura, I was wrong."

She shrugged. "About which thing, Bash?"

"I tried to tell myself that our lives would be easier and less complicated if we weren't together. It was lazy and it was wrong."

"Whatever. You had a whole list of reasons you didn't want to be with me. Are you saying you just changed your mind and now I'm *worthy* all of a sudden? You can *deal* with me now? You said I was—"

"I know the stupid shit that I said!" He caught himself yelling and softened his tone. "Baby, all I can say now is that I screwed up." His shoulders sagged and he played with the cord on her blinds to avoid looking her in the face. "I saw you with him and I know I'm probably too late but I had to find out if we still have chance in hell at making this work."

She gave him a grim look, admitting, "You were right about me."

He panicked, praying it wasn't about Andrew. "About which thing?"

"It turns out I'm much darker and messier than you ever imagined."

Relief washed over him, and he touched her chin. "If you're talking about your dad, we've met." He tapped the bandage on his head. "That was no gas leak. By the way, guess where you get your fiery talents from?"

Her fingers tingled and panic swept through her body. "Sebastian, you have to get away from me right now. He's going after the ones we love. God, I should have known."

She grabbed her phone. "Brian…"

"He doesn't want Brian." He tried to keep her calm as she dialed. "I don't know why, he specifically mentioned it though."

After confirming her son's safety, she opened the door for Bash to leave, but he took her by the arm, pulled her inside and closed it.

She jerked free and pushed him in the chest. "I said get away from me!"

He crushed her arms to her sides and said, "Laura, we are not doing this."

She struggled against him, but he put her against the wall and pinned her arms over her head. Trying to keep his voice steady, he argued, "If you want to throw me out, do it because I'm an asshole, not because you're afraid for me."

She twisted in his grasp, so he used his hips to push her back. "Dammit woman, I'm not running away from this, and I'm not running away from you ever again."

All of the possible scenarios raced through her mind. Would their love be a death sentence for him? Thomas wasn't likely to let it go if he'd already tried to kill him once. Would Bash be any safer on his own than with her? No, they were better together, and she'd always known it. It was he who couldn't figure that out. He'd tripped all over his emotions and made them both suffer but the hope in his eyes was melting her heart.

The veins in his arms protruded as his muscles flexed to hold her in place, and he pleaded, "Tell me what you really want."

In truth, he'd done what she wanted just by coming to her door. They were sure to have a rough time, but she knew they could make it so the reality was that she would never send him away. Her breathing steadied, and she relaxed under his grip.

"I want you to stay."

He rested his forehead to hers and she felt the tension in his body melt away. They breathed into each other, passion swelling in the space between them.

She pressed her inner thigh to his. "I want..."

He nuzzled her ear and murmured, "What else do you want, baby?"

"I want to feel you inside me."

He released her arms and moved his hands to her face, bringing her mouth to his and hungrily searching for her tongue. She nibbled at his bottom lip and curled a finger through his belt loop, pulling their hips together.

He tugged on a fistful of her hair, exposing her throat to his kisses. The feel of his lips on her neck sent waves of yearning through her body and her fingers eagerly pulled at the buttons on his jeans.

As she stroked him, he groaned and let his head fall back against the wall. "I am so hard for you, Laura."

He ran his hands down her back and over her bottom, lifting her as she wrapped her legs around his waist. He carried her down the hall and, in the bedroom, laid her down and pulled off his shirt. When she tugged his jeans over his hips and ran her tongue above the waistband of his boxer briefs, his boot got stuck on his heel and he fell in a powerless heap on the bed. "You are driving me wild."

She stood up with a smirk, and said, "Let me help."

After wrestling off his jeans, she stepped out of her shorts and crawled next to him. His fingers travelled from between her legs to under her top and back, teasing her until she begged for him.

He whisked off the tank and grimaced. Since the last thing he wanted to do was hurt her, he shoved a pillow under her hips so he could hover over her wounded belly and then they both gasped as he slid inside her. She gripped his shoulders and arched her body to meet his powerful thrusts and he lowered his head to roll his tongue across her nipples until she cried out and pulled him to her, sinking her teeth into the compass tattoo on his chest.

When he could feel her body quiver, he let himself lose control. She clenched her muscles around him, and he came so hard that for a second, he thought Laura might have saved Thomas the trouble of taking him out.

When they caught their breath, Laura ran her finger along the arrows in his tattoo and made a face. "Eeesh, I left a mark."

He propped himself on an elbow and grinned. "You can chew on me all you want, I love it."

He was bleeding through the bandage over his eye, so she moved to get supplies, but he held her down and nodded at the slashes across her stomach.

"When you tell me about that."

She plucked his button down off the floor and busied herself with putting it on to avoid the question.

His body was starting to rebel against the events of the last twenty-four hours. Every muscle was sore, his head was throbbing, and he was starving. All he wanted to do was eat a pizza, then sleep in her arms for about three days, but if they were to survive, he needed to know what happened to her and what she knew about Thomas.

"Please," he said, grazing his fingers across her knee, "talk to me."

He had promised not to run again, but what she had to say would be one hell of a test. She took a deep breath, looked him in the face, and told him everything. She told him about the demon they thought was a ghost, the meeting with the Other Side, her failure with the spell, Adira's revenge, meeting Thomas, and her fight with Sarah. She even mentioned Brona's appearance right before his arrival that night.

He curled his lip and looked around the room as if the demon might pop out any minute, and Laura bopped the tip of his nose with her finger. "That's why Drew's been hanging around so much more. He's our friend, and he's helping us with things like research and moral support."

Bash rolled his eyes and put his hands behind his head.

Her tone sobered again. "It won't get any easier, Sebastian. We've been playing dial a disaster for a year now and it's all finally starting to make sense. If that guy is an angel from Hell, and if he is my father..."

He gave her a crooked grin. "That makes you half angel and I could have told you that all along." He sat up and took her hands in his. "Look at me. He might have plans for you, but it's not up to him. No one is born evil, baby. You made your choice long before he showed up."

His stomach growled, and she shimmied her shoulders at him, purring, I have pizza in the fridge."

## Chapter Sixteen

Earlier that night, Bob Mercer walked the floor in his garage. There was something he had to do, and it was so important. The tickle in his brain, just outside his awareness, was driving him mad. He'd moved things around and parked his pickup in the garage, giving himself until seven o'clock to remember. He paced until the soles of his shoes wore thin and at 6:55, he banged his forehead against the side door. What was it?

He could almost see it, but it disappeared again. At 6:57, he banged his head on the door until the wood cracked from the force of the blows and at seven o'clock, he climbed in the truck and started the engine. The blood burned as it ran into his eyes, so he closed them and leaned back against the seat, remembering that he'd read somewhere that it wouldn't take very long.

A few minutes later, the garage door lifted enough for the dog to scoot underneath. It latched its jaws on to the leg of Bob's jeans, pulling him away from the danger. Bob's head rolled around, but there was just a blur of teeth and after a moment of confusion, the dog came into focus, and he tried to sit up. The carbon monoxide had begun to permeate his tissues, so his movements were sluggish and heavy as he slid out of the vehicle.

"Where is he?" he asked the dog.

The garage door completed its track to the ceiling and Thomas strode past him to turn off the engine. He stuffed a bandana in Bob's hand and clicked his tongue.

"Bob, you weren't trying to get out of your assignment, were you?"

Bob dabbed at his forehead and cried out in frustration. "Tell me you remember what I'm supposed to do!"

"Of course, I remember." Thomas gave the dog an exasperated look. "Go to the college, Bob. Find Audra Deane and bring her to me."


The parking lot at Tri-Cities Community College wasn't well lit on a clear night, let alone during a dust storm. Audi was cautious most of the time, but the professor had kept them late, and she was disheveled. Her backpack hung open, and she was juggling her water bottle while digging the keys out of her purse as the wind plastered her hair to her face. She could smell moisture in the air and imagined she and Noah would rock his truck in the rain after his shift, if only she could get a move on.

Her latest crush was a burly paramedic with a sleeve of Celtic tattoos who spoke on the class Discord almost entirely in Rick and Morty memes. Noah enrolled in the nursing program in anticipation of the inevitable paramedic burnout and the promise of a more lucrative second career.

But Bob Mercer crouched in the back seat of her ancient Toyota, running his finger along the blade of the K-Bar and wondering if Sheriff Scott would approve of his knife choice.

She threw her stuff on the passenger side and clicked the seat belt in a huff. When the door slammed, Bob sprang forward and grabbed her. She jerked away and tried to kick open the door, but he pulled her seatbelt tight and pressed his knife to the side of her head. She struggled and screamed but the few students in the parking lot were rushing to their cars to escape the dust storm.

"What do you want?" She gasped, finally.

"You're going to drive."

"No fucking way."

He moved the knife lower and pushed it to her throat. She'd always mocked girls who were kidnapped on cop shows. How could they be so stupid? Why didn't they fight? Everyone knows you don't let him take you anywhere. You certainly don't drive yourself to your own murder scene.

In that moment, she knew exactly how it could happen. She was so afraid that panic tunneled her vision, and she could feel her heart beating in her chest. Extending her arm, she used her power to fling the water bottle at her attacker, but she couldn't see him, and it bounced off his shoulder.

"Crazy witch." He grabbed the rest of her things and pulled them on to the seat next to him.

Her phone was in her purse and the old car had no GPS. Half of her brain told her to stay put. *Make him kill you right there if that's what he wants to do.* The other half was screaming, *Just do what he says!*

She pulled the car toward the lot exit. "You got an address, asshole?"

"Head west and I'll tell you where to turn. It's not that far."

She paused on the brake, so he jerked on her seatbelt again. "What are you waiting for?"

She yelped and fresh tears spilled down her cheeks. "I don't know west."

"Turn right, you stupid girl."

*Oh, God.* He was taking her to the mountains. The hiking trails were closed and the road was deserted. If he got her alone out there…

She stole a glance in the review mirror and recognized him in an instant. "Mr. Mercer? What the hell are you doing?"

She suddenly remembered the Sheriff's ramblings at Laura's house. He'd said Mercer was unstable and might have murdered David Martin.

His eyes definitely had a crazy look when they met hers in the reflection. "Just drive."

The wind was so strong she could barely keep her little car on the road and when several large raindrops plopped onto the windshield, she smiled to herself.

Giant Cottonwood trees lined that stretch of Olive Road and they'd been getting quite a bit of unusual weather lately, so it was slick and lined with puddles. She slowed the car a bit and stole another glance at him. He was directly behind her, but that was fine. The trees were on the right and the rain was starting to pour. *Perfect.*

"Hey, I didn't tell you to stop." He pressed on the knife for emphasis.

"You're the boss." She steered to the right and pressed her foot to the floor. As she'd hoped, the car began to slide to the left, so she cranked the wheel into the skid, sending the back end of the car into the base of one of the biggest trees. The airbag exploded into her face, throwing her backward, and Bob Mercer flew across the back seat, his body hitting the door at the same time as the tree.

As she lost consciousness, a random grateful thought floated through mind. *Thank you, B.R.A.K.E.S. driving school.*

Laura woke to the sound of Sebastian rummaging around in the kitchen. She stretched long and savored a few memories from the night before until she caught a good look at the bed. Between the wounds on her belly and his, well, everywhere, the sheets were streaked with blood and gave the room the feel of crime scene.

A few minutes later, she stood measuring bleach over the washing machine and mulling over events from the day before. Great sex and a good night's sleep had improved her perspective enough that she was no longer sure the entire business had been a failure.

Adira said the demon was their own splendid creation. The mountain lion had genuinely wondered why they would want to destroy it. Why indeed?

She found Bash puzzling over the Nespresso machine. He'd pulled on his jeans but was barefoot and shirtless. His back was thick with muscle but also swollen, cut, and bruised from the night before.

Quelling the urge to find Thomas that instant and make him pay, she instead ran a gentle finger down her lover's spine.

He waved his hand over the coffee maker. "When did you get this thing?"

"It was a broken heart present to me."

"Well," he winced, "I tried, but I guess you'll have to show me what to do here."

She wrapped her arms around his neck. "Your skills lie in *other* areas."

He kissed her long and slow, then tore himself away to collect their phones. "I'm gonna check on Chuck."

As the men spoke, their voices faded, and Sarah's presence invaded Laura's consciousness. When her phone rang, her sister's voice was strained with worry.

"There's been a car accident. Audi is in the Emergency Room. Laura, Bob Mercer tried to kidnap her."

When she hung up Bash was pulling on his t-shirt. "Did she say Bob Mercer?"

Laura swiped some jeans from a drawer. "You know Thomas is behind this."

He clenched his jaw. "Oh, yeah, that mother fucker is on a roll."

The free-standing Emergency Room was located just on the outskirts of Chuparosa and since Audi was the only patient at the time, the triage nurse ushered them back right away.

Audi's eyes were black and her head bobbed under the weight of the pain medication. When they arrived, she was sitting up talking to her parents, or rather, they were talking to her.

She gave Laura a sloppy wave and fell over. "Aunteeee."

Rueben met them at the door. "Sheriff, they transported Mercer somewhere in Phoenix-I guess he's in bad shape. What did he want with my girl?"

Laura left them, kissed Audi's cheek, and hugged Sarah. They held each other tightly until Drew walked in with two drink carriers full of coffee.

He set one down in front of Bash and said, "I thought you guys could use this."

Rueben reached for a cup. "He's right about that. Preachers always seem to know exactly when they're needed."

Bash gritted his teeth as Laura waved Drew over, "Especially that one."

"I called him on our way and told him everything," Laura explained to Sarah. "I also checked on Brian and he's okay for now."

Sarah took a coffee and furrowed her brow. "Brian? What are you talking about?" She looked Laura up and down. "And what are you wearing?"

Laura gazed down at Bash's shirt and shrugged.

"Ahhh, nice!" Audi slurred. "Auntie got railed."

Sarah squeezed her daughter's hand. "Audra, please. Wait, did you?"

Laura raised her eyebrows, "Is that what they're calling it now? Good God."

Drew bowed his head to hide a smile. If there was a railing, that meant Bash had come to his senses and, more importantly, that Laura welcomed him back. At least one act of their shit show had some promise.

Sarah's protective instincts had been in high gear since dawn and she narrowed her eyes. "Where is he?"

"Relax. He came over last night after Thomas tried to blow him up."

"What?"

Laura ran her fingers through Audi's hair and tilted her head toward Bash. "Thomas is using them to get to us."

A nurse made her way through the crowd to take Audi's vital signs. She sneered and pushed by Drew, so he took Laura and Sarah by the arms and walked them to the door.

"Not one of us is on the same page right now, so we better sit down and talk."

Bash couldn't argue with that, and he led the group to the tiny cafeteria at the other end of the facility.

As they situated themselves, Drew leaned against the vending machine and surveyed the other men. Sebastian was uncomfortable and needed a job to do. He kept checking his phone for news from Chuck and hovering in support with his hand on Laura's back.

Rueben gestured angrily, storming around and barking at Sarah. If she cried, Drew knew he wouldn't be able to stop himself from punching her husband and completely upending their friendship. That wasn't Sarah's way though, and it was entirely possible she would knock him out herself.

It was Laura, surprising no one, who positioned herself nose to nose with Rueben. "Watch your tone," she warned him.

Bash was then tasked with keeping her from committing assault and Drew was thrust back into his role of pastor. "Let's everyone focus on our real problems, okay?"

Bash had seen Drew watching Sarah though, and it didn't take him five seconds to realize that it wasn't Laura he wanted after all. He'd always grudgingly respected the man, but for the first time Bash looked on Drew with real compassion. The ramifications of the preacher's feelings were likely to be painful and disappointing at best, and Bash could only imagine how awful and conflicted he felt. *Poor bastard.*

## Chapter Seventeen

Sarah excused herself and the janitor mopping the entryway pointed her to the restroom. The overhead light popped and flickered when the door closed behind her, but she didn't give it much thought as she stared into the mirror and let the cool water run over her hands.

On any other day she might have been irritated when Laura stepped in, but it wouldn't hurt Rueben at all to deal with her older sister. The look on Bash's face when she'd poked Rueben in the chest made it worth it anyway. Laura kept everyone on their toes and Sarah had to acknowledge that it wasn't always a bad thing.

Her sister's big heart kept them from getting rid of the Brona demon, but no one loved like Laura did. Sebastian would pay dearly if he hurt her a second time and Sarah vowed to herself that it would be the most potent spell she ever worked. As far as Rueben was concerned, the Brona demon was right. She'd married someone just like her father, or the man she thought was her father, and she unexpectedly sympathized with her mother for the first time in her life.

Soap spewed from the dispenser when she bent to splash water on her face and, when she moved away from the motion detector, it didn't stop. The dispenser on the other sink sputtered and spewed, then both faucets began rapidly filling the sinks.

Sarah pounded the wall in annoyance. "Just show yourself already."

The light fixture hummed and popped and began to rain sparks, then all three stall doors swung open with a deafening bang. She whirled around to see Brona leaning against the main door, smiling a wicked smile.

Sarah threw her hand into the air, slamming the stall doors shut with her power. "This is getting really old," she grumbled.

"I warned you about him," the Brona demon snarked, "but you were so stubborn."

Sarah marched over and went nose to nose with her, the way Laura had done with Rueben, and hissed, "I would have done anything to get away from you."

She was angry but also getting nervous as the sinks overflowed to a puddle of water on the floor that began inching its way toward the spray of electricity.

Someone pressed the door from the outside, but Brona held it closed with her weight. "What will you do now? You're already forty-seven years old so you should probably just plan to die alone like I did."

That was actually one of Sarah's greatest fears. She put her hands over her ears and yelled, "Stop!"

The door pushed against Brona once more and this time she heard her sister's call. The lights popped again, and the water seeped closer to her sandals as Laura burst through the door sending Brona's body to the floor.

"Wait!" Sarah pointed to the light fixture.

Laura looked up and then to the water on the floor and smiled. A thought she considered in the laundry room earlier occurred to her again and she took a tentative step into the water. Sarah yelped another warning, but Laura held a hand up in reassurance.

Shockwaves ran up her legs and her heart might have skipped a few beats but as suspected she remained mostly unharmed. In fact, she was able to isolate the power flowing into her body long enough to hurl the demon across the floor in a burst of blue light.

She held her arms out to Sarah and said, "Jump."

Brona stretched out to grab her ankle but Sarah jerked it away and leapt for her sister just as the puddle reached her and they fell together on the floor just outside the bathroom door.

The triage nurse ran and knelt beside them. "Good Lord, what happened in there?"

Laura moved the janitor's caution cone in front of the bathroom door and said calmly, "You have a leak and a bad light bulb."

Back in the cafeteria, Rueben pulled a napkin from the dispenser and handed it to Sarah while Bash and Drew exchanged confused glances but said nothing.

Sarah snatched the napkin from Rueben and wiped her face. "We need to work fast."

Drew pulled several books from his satchel and dropped them on the table. "I've learned some things about Thomas," he began, "if I'm right, he was what God called a Watcher angel named Thamuz. I think the reason he didn't kill me the other day is that he's more powerful at night. I mean, he could have killed me, and we know he wanted to, but I don't believe he could have successfully fought the three of you afterward."

Again, Bash cursed himself for not being there that day. He sifted through Drew's books and held up The Complete Idiots Guide to Angels. "Are you fucking kidding me?"

"It's an incredibly valuable resource," Drew said, unfazed by his mocking, "Thomas told us about his first children, and he was probably referring to the Nephilim." He took the book from Bash and flipped to a dog-eared page.

"This says that certain angels-Watchers-were charged with taking care of the humans after they were kicked out of Eden. But the angels got bored and started teaching the humans about magic and war, *and* they had children with them."

Bash furrowed his brows. "The Nephilim?"

"Yes, but they were enormous, violent, grotesque, creatures that God wiped out in the flood."

Noah's flood?" Rueben's face twisted in disbelief. "Are you people insane?"

Bash moved between them and draped an arm around each sister's waist. "Okay, but they're not grotesque. Not even close."

"A fair amount of evolution has taken place since then, and we just don't know—"

A few people wandered in from the waiting room, so Rueben shushed him. "We're getting weird looks so let's take this to the house."

Back in Audi's room, they found Noah bent over her bed in the middle of a kiss. Rueben shot Bash and Drew an irritated look and clapped his hands. "Hey!"

Noah emitted an odd squeak and stood at attention as Bash laughed and nudged him out. "Come with us, kid."

Audi would be okay, but the doctor wanted to keep her under observation until the next morning, for which Sarah was grateful. She would, hopefully, be out of harm's way while she was there.

They decided to gather in the desert behind Sarah's house where they could spread out and talk freely. Rueben glared a dangerous warning at Noah once more and, to the nurses' relief, they left as a group.

At home, Sarah handed Rueben a cold water bottle and pressed one to her forehead. "Can you believe that in the middle of all this, my sister is falling in love?"

"Well," Rueben scoffed, "that's a disaster waiting to happen."

She slammed the water bottle on the counter. "Why? Because they're not afraid to admit their mistakes? Because they're passionate and fearless?"

"I was going to say because he's a hot head and she's crazy, but…"

"They let themselves have feelings. Is that a crime? Maybe just in this house."

"Are we gonna do this right now?"

"Why not, Rueben? You don't touch me, you barely speak to me, and now you're in danger because of me. This is your chance, your excuse, to walk away. You better do it now before shit really hits the fan."

"Is that what you think I want?" He caught the reflection of himself in the patio door glass, the reflection of a man he no longer recognized. Over the years, he'd convinced himself that she was different than the girl he fell in love with. He blamed her changing hormones for making her sentimental but deep inside, he knew the issues were mainly his. The more he pulled away, the harder she worked to pull him back. She wasn't just being sentimental; she was trying to save their marriage.

"I got old Sarah," he sighed, "I knew you were unhappy, but I got old and tired, and I guess I quit trying."

She rested her hand over his heart and asked, "Did you quit caring?"

"No. But I don't know where we go from here."

She reached for him, and he pulled her into his arms. He hadn't held her like that in years and the foreign feel of his embrace was too much for Sarah. Pent up emotion spilled out of her in waves until she found herself sobbing uncontrollably.

He only then realized the depth of his wife's misery. "I love you," he said, hoping he wasn't too late. "We'll figure this out, I promise."


When not on the clock, Bash drove a midnight black Toyota Tundra, though the July heat provided him with a cruel reminder every summer why one should not buy black vehicles in Arizona. Even so, it was his favorite possession.

Experiences from his younger days left him with certain insecurities that, on the right day, could wrestle him to the ground. Those matches grew less frequent as he aged, but it gave him strange comfort to know if things ever really went sideways in his cherished

Chuparosa, he could leave everything and go anywhere in the truck.

Laura loved his truck, too, particularly sitting up high in the passenger seat next to him. One of her favorite memories was an ill-thought-out attempt at sex in the front seat after an evening hike in the mountains. They might have felt like kids at the onset but when Bash got a cramp in his side, the violent contortion of his body caused her head to bounce off the dashboard. The whole incident ended with him doubled over outside and with her crumpled on the floorboard of the passenger seat, both of them wheezing with laughter. Since then they still managed plenty of foreplay in the truck on dark dirt roads but decided to accept that their ages did carry certain limitations.

Their circumstances were dire, but Laura was happy to be riding next to him again. Her mood soured as they pulled into Sarah's driveway, though. Her sister could hide a breakdown from the others, but she would never be fooled, and she knew it was Rueben's fault.

She hopped out and balled her fists. "What did he do?"

Andrew was pulling up as well, so Sarah waved her off. "We'll talk about it later."

Bash hung up his phone and announced, "Chuck's arm will take about six weeks to heal, but otherwise, he's in good shape. He put the two of us on medical leave for a few days."

Andrew grabbed his backpack and slammed the door to his 4Runner. "Then, let's get this figured out."

The plan was to hike a half-mile or so to Sarah's favorite spot with shade and flat rocks where they could spread out and talk. They trekked in silence until Laura noticed a shimmer in the sand ahead. The figure of a man appeared on the edge of the canyon's ridge with his back to them. He wore khaki pants and hiking boots but carried no water or backpack.

Laura veered toward him. "Stupid tourist, he's going to fall."

Bash trailed her and hollered, "Hey, Indiana Jones, you're too close to the edge!"

"I could say the same thing about you, Sebastian."

The man had dark wavy hair like Thomas, but it was cut shorter in a corporate looking style. When he turned to face them, his porcelain skin glowed luminescent in the sunlight. It was Drew who noticed the elaborate markings on his arms, like the marks on Thomas, but flesh colored, not dark and scarlike.

"Guys, get back," he warned.

When Laura tried to move away, the man jerked her up by the arm and held her to the edge of the cliff. He towered over her, and her feet dangled several inches above the ground. At his touch, the strength left her body as if a tap had been opened and she slumped in his grasp.

"Let her go, god dammit!" Bash drew his gun and cocked the hammer.

"Whoa, whoa, whoa!" Drew threw his hands up and stood between them. "Who are you? What do you want from us?"

Rueben tried to push Sarah behind him, but she shoved him away and said, "Lolly, hang on."

Wings unfurled behind the man, soft and gray, like the ones Bash had seen on Thomas. He shook Laura and frowned at the others. "I want you to know where you stand with me."

Bash inched closer to him and snarled, "I've seen angel wings before, and they don't impress me. I swear I will kill you."

Drew pulled his own gun and stood at Bash's side. "I said, who are you?"

The angel's face softened a bit and for the first time they could see his eyes, ice blue, like Sarah's.

"I'm Daniel. And you, Andrew, are out of your depth."

Daniel brought Laura to Bash and released her. She shuddered and fell into his arms, struggling for air.

"You're like Thomas, but you're not from Hell," she gasped, "I can feel it."

Her power had surged when Thomas touched her, but Daniel sapped it from her.

"Thomas is not from Hell either, Laura."

Sarah knelt to relieve Bash, who stood and retrained his gun on Daniel's chest. Just an hour ago, she'd told Rueben that things couldn't get any worse, but now cursed herself for tempting fate. "We already have an angel, so you can go." She said.

"I'm afraid that's exactly why I'm planning to stay." Daniel dropped a smooth black stone on the ground next to Laura that emitted a violet glow around her body.

Drew lowered his gun. "If you're an angel from Heaven, aren't you supposed to be telling us not to be afraid?"

"Oh, no. You'd better be afraid of me."

Laura hauled herself up and dusted off her jeans. "Why am I not surprised that *we* don't get a guardian angel?"

Rueben sat down on a rock and shook his head at Daniel, "Man, it has been a long ass day, can you just explain yourself? Please?"

Daniel had been offended by their disrespect but had to admit that since Thomas was their first angelic encounter, they weren't likely to trust him either. He was not one for explaining himself, but a change in demeanor seemed appropriate in order to make them understand the gravity of their situation. He gave them what he hoped was a patient smile and did as Rueben asked.

"I'm more like your Governor, Laura. There are beings on this earth that shouldn't exist—"

"Like us," Sarah rolled her eyes, "we're aware, thanks."

"It's my job to monitor such beings."

"Ha," Laura interrupted, "like a zookeeper? Fuck you."

Drew moved in front of her and rubbed at his ribcage, recalling how Thomas had reacted to that kind of stubbornness, but she pushed around him.

"If you're supposed to be policing things that shouldn't exist," she argued, "we've been picking up a lot of your slack, pal."

"My only concerns right now are you and your sister. I don't know why yet, but Thomas wants your power and the current running through this town," Daniel replied.

Sarah laughed. "Your timing is awful. You really want help from a couple of cranky, peri-menopausal women?"

Again, they'd surprised him, and Daniel found himself getting defensive, a state of affairs that could only lead to another failure. So, he folded away his wings and tried yet another tactic to reach them.

"Your concept of time and age are deeply flawed. The human obsession with youth is impractical and frankly, bizarre. The fear of aging is what ultimately keeps a woman from fully developing all of her spiritual powers."

"Thomas spent hundreds of years trying to create sons with the perfect balance of strength and magical ability. He was chasing the wrong kind of strength though, and he's finally figured that out. Don't you see? It's in these decades after fertility that you will become more valuable to him than ever."

Drew shared a nervous glance with the other men. Nothing good could come from being valuable to Thomas. "But there's no evil here," he stressed the word 'no', "only magic."

"There's also tremendous passion and depth of feeling," Daniel said, admitting it to himself for the first time. "That makes you vulnerable and I've no doubt Thomas sees unlimited potential here. You created your own demon, after all."

"If your job is to keep these "beings" in check," Bash wondered, "why don't you just kill Thomas?"

"That's not how it works. His Governor was…destroyed. By the way, your weapon won't work on me, Sebastian. You already knew that, so you might as well put it away."

He was right but though Bash knew it, he kept his gun drawn out of obstinance. "This Governor of his…he had no partner? No backup? You can't just step in and take over?"

"Humans have that kind of potential, but angels have singular purpose."

Sarah's anger bloomed fresh. "If we're your purpose, why did you let that maniac take my daughter?"

Daniel rested his gaze on Bash. "I was needed elsewhere."

At once, the odd events at the Sheriff's station began to make sense and Bash said, "That's why we weren't killed in the blast. You bastard." He ran a shaky hand through his hair. "We could have lost the kid."

"She's one of them Sebastian and they are expendable, but you are essential to the bigger picture."

Laura sniffed. "You were sent to kill us, so it makes sense. Why not have Bob Mercer do your dirty work?"

"I had nothing to do with that."

The women shrank away from him as he made his way back to the canyon ridge and he was torn over whether that made him feel better or worse.

"Don't misunderstand me. I'm not your enemy, "he explained before he disappeared, "but the choices you make going forward will have a direct impact on mine."

## Chapter Eighteen

They returned to Sarah's house with more questions than answers, but the immediate way forward was clear, and she was determined. "The first thing we have to do is get rid of the Brona demon. We can't fight her and Thomas at the same time."

Laura dragged her foot across the doormat. "About that..."

"No, Laura. Let's cut the cord just like we planned. It's been part of me for way too long."

"What if we were able to break the curse and take back the power we gave it? Remember, I already started in the bathroom at the ER."

Sarah tossed a couple of bags of chips to the men leaning on her kitchen counters and reminded her, "We're the curse, remember?"

Drew ripped open some Doritos. "I have to agree with Laura on this. It's been gorging on you and making you weaker. You've always tried to keep a lid on your powers, but what if you didn't?"

"Preacher, I don't think that's helpful," Rueben protested.

Bash rubbed Laura's shoulders. Though it pained him, he had to admit that Drew was right. What would happen if Lura were ever truly backed into a corner, or if someone tried to hurt Brian? How much power had she been keeping suppressed? What was she capable of? Did she even know? There was a time when he would have preferred not to ask but he'd evolved quite a bit over the last few hours. The stronger she and Sarah were, the better everyone's chances of surviving. Surviving Thomas, anyway.

"If you go for it, baby, go all the way. Don't just absorb this thing, embrace it all."

Sarah picked at her thumbnail. "If this gets out of hand, Daniel will kill us on principle."

Laura sniffed and stuck her hand in Bash's bag of barbecue chips. "Daniel and his sketchy principles can—"

"Do you forgive her?" Sarah interrupted.

Drew could sense the kitchen closing in with emotion, so he swiped the canister labeled "Salt" from the counter and led the other men to the sunroom. Bash and Rueben gaped as he gave the coffee table a shove and poured a circle on the carpet.

"You're gonna have to trust me on this one."

Laura hoisted herself up on the island. She could not imagine the chain of events that led her mother into Thomas' trap. More so, she couldn't fathom why Brona turned on the only two people who could have appreciated her dilemma. The woman had never shared her story with them or even spoken to them like human beings. Resentment backed up into her throat. *What a team they could have made.*

"We don't have to forgive her; we don't even have to try to understand. We'll just take back what's ours."

Water bubbled up through the drain while Sarah contemplated. At last, she raised her chin. "Then let's do it. Now."

"Wait." Rueben was tense. "How do you know it will just show up?"

Sarah moved away from the window as the curtains began to flutter in wind that wasn't there, and Laura lit a burner on the stove to scoop some flame into her hand.

"It's always with us."

Outside, the wind grew stronger, putting a bend in the trees, their branches scraping against the side of the house.

Rueben closed the patio door and for a second seemed pleased with himself as he said, "I knew it was too early for the monsoon."

Without fanfare, the Brona demon appeared seated at the kitchen table tapping her fingernails on the wood.

Bash jerked his head back in surprise. "Woah." Neither he nor Rueben had seen it before. "They think that's their mother?"

Drew nudged them into the circle. "It's complicated."

Thunder cracked outside and the lights flickered over the table. Laura tossed bits of flame, lighting the candles situated around the various rooms and leaned on her elbows, facing the demon.

"Show yourself," she demanded.

The Brona demon began to change before her. Tapping fingernails became scratching talons while its torso lengthened into sinews atop thin legs with hoofed feet.

Her breath caught in her throat as the horror she'd created became clear to her at last. She was appalled but found herself intrigued as well. *Who knew?*

She leaned close to the demon's face and said, "You're coming with us."

A cookbook flew across the room and hit her in the back, causing her to fall to her to her knees.

Bash lurched for her, but Drew held him back, saying, "It's not our fight."

The demon left the table and scraped across the floor. "I go where I want, witch."

Sarah backed against the stove and Laura could tell by the look on her face that she still couldn't see it.

"Sarah, you know it's not Mom. Look at it, look hard. The only one bringing her into this is you."

Sarah's chin trembled. Thomas and Daniel had confirmed for them what Brona always said. They were abominations, damned things, and she was afraid.

"She left us with this Lolly. She just left us."

There could not have been a more inconvenient moment for her sister to find her feelings. Even so, Laura had known for a long time that it was going to happen, and that it would be grisly when it did.

"She was never really there, Sarah."

Sarah had always envied Laura's ability to accept her fate. She had an unquenchable thirst for understanding, but not about the afterlife. In the absence of an explanation from her mother, Laura simply lived her life, unapologetic for its origins even after they learned about Thomas.

Like Brona, Sarah always looked to the church for redemption. While Brona sought forgiveness for the choices made by a desperate teenager, Sarah sought to salvage a life forsaken in which the choices were never even hers to make.

She whirled on the demon, who still appeared to her as her mother, and tears spilled down her cheeks. "Why didn't you tell us?"

Lightning struck a Chinaberry tree in the backyard, splitting it down the middle. One side crashed through the patio door, separating the men from Laura and Sarah. Sheets of rain beat the floor and the counters, and electricity popped from every appliance.

Drew felt the hair on his arms raise and pulled Bash out of the circle and on to the couch with him to avoid electrocution. He called for Rueben to joint them, but Sarah's husband ran out the door.

"You made me so afraid." Sarah said, advancing on the demon.

Its talons reached out to welcome her with a deadly hug and Laura knew it would rip her to shreds if she didn't wake up to reality.

"Sarah! Just look at it!"

"You made me afraid of myself, but I wasn't the real monster, was I?"

Sarah ducked out of the way as the demon swiped at her and Laura blew a sigh of relief. She was beginning to see the ugliness and outrage they'd manifested into talons, hooves, and claws.

It occurred to Sarah that fear was both her mother's weapon and her weakness. She and her sister were powerful beings who should strike fear in their enemies, not cower away from them. If they were damned, then so be it.

She reached out with her mind and forced the demon against the wall. She could not right Brona's wrongs, but she could right plenty of others. It would require her to embrace her true nature and, she cast a glance at Andrew, require that she reorder her future.

The demon hissed and lumbered toward the women. Laura's flame had been extinguished by the rain, so she snatched some electricity from the air, rolling it back and forth through her hands until it grew into a sizeable ball.

Since Bash had seen first-hand what Thomas could do with a ball of lightning, he told Drew to brace himself. He also told himself it was perfectly fine that Laura, the woman he loved, could throw a power bomb, just like her dad, an angel from Hell. Since he was also quite familiar with the strength behind her windup, he pushed the two of them deeper into the cushions.

At that moment, Sarah had never been more sure of her own resolve, but Laura made her nervous.

"Can you do it? Can you kill our mother?"

Laura narrowed her eyes and said, "That's not our mother."

She rolled the power around in her hands, then reared back and threw it at the demon's feet. Sarah grabbed her and they charged through the light, crashing into the cabinets as they tackled it.

The demon fell atop the sisters, howling and clawing at them to get away. They held on tight and the intensity of its slashes against their skin lessened as it liquified and dissolved into their bodies. Smoke rose from the wood as residual current crackled across the floor and into the felled tree, frying the leaves off its branches into crispy piles on the floor. When the air cleared, Laura and Sarah lay soaked and unmoving.

"Sarah!" Drew lunged for her, but Bash pulled him back.

"Hold on!" Rueben shouted from outside. He'd been waiting by the breaker box. "Okay, it's safe now!"

As Sarah tried to stand, Rueben picked her up and carried her to the chaise in the sunroom.

Drew regretted his indiscretion at once, and covered his face with his hands, whispering, "God help me," to himself.

Bash slid through the water on his knees to scooped Laura into his arms. "Baby? Talk to me."

She couldn't find her voice yet but smiled weakly and buried her head in his chest. He pulled her closer, squeezing his eyes tight to shut out the preacher's pain.

After they chain sawed the tree and boarded up the door, everyone went their separate ways for some well-deserved downtime. Sarah checked in with Audi and found herself alone, again.

She took a long shower and climbed naked into bed, full of energy with no outlet for it. While digging around in the bedside drawer for the sedative Laura made for her, she felt Rueben's fingers graze her hip. It startled her so badly that she jumped out of bed.

"Jesus, Rueben, you scared me to death."

He reached for her again as she climbed back under the sheets and, after a moment, it dawned on her what he was up to, but the shock made her quite numb for a few seconds.

He smoothed the hair from her face and let his fingers linger on her throat. His voice was hoarse and a bit hesitant, but he said, "I want you, Sarah."

Her first instinct was to put her back to him. *Too little, too late, sir.* But her shoulders softened away from her ears as she caught something in the droop of his eyes that pulled up a memory of their first time. She lifted her lips to his tentative kisses, kisses that grew deeper and firmer as she arched into him.

They were clumsy and awkward at first, but he soon remembered just how to touch her. As his hands slid along her curves it didn't take long for them to find their rhythm. She'd craved that closeness for so long, and he'd forgotten how good it felt to hear her call out his name.

Laura woke early and watched Bash while he slept. Daniel could praise the aging process as much as he wanted but they were all cresting a half-a-century. Whether they were in decent shape or not, they didn't feel like superheroes, especially when they were fighting bad guys.

When she brushed her fingers through the salt and pepper at his temples, he opened his eyes and gave her a sleepy smile. "What are you thinking, baby?"

"I'm glad you were there."

He pulled her into his arms and said, "I need you to promise me something."

She reached up touched his face. "I promise to love this beard you're growing."

"I'm serious. Promise you'll never try to keep me safe."

She furrowed her brows. "What?"

"I mean it, Laura. Don't lie to protect me, don't put yourself in extra danger for me, none of that. Don't you dare. I know I almost ruined everything, but it took me nearly fifty years to find you and I won't live without you now. I won't do it. Do you understand what I'm saying? If it comes to that, I'm your partner and I'm going with you. Promise me."

"Sebastian…"

"Promise me."

She supposed that if the tables were turned, she would have made the same request of him. They were far from the perfect couple but something in her knew that somehow, they would be together until they died. The ease with which she made the decision didn't give her the slightest pang of guilt. She would do that for him, for them.

"Alright. I promise."

## Chapter Nineteen

When he left, Laura opened up the living room armoire and gathered some supplies. Her intention flowed through the room as she selected the items she would need to help keep him safe. He'd made her promise not to risk herself without taking him along, but it wasn't a suicide pact.

As far as she knew, both of them would just as soon leave Hell's angel to those better suited for the fight. If Daniel's pal, with the power of Heaven behind him, had already failed, she didn't know how he expected *them* to pull it off.

Still, something in her thrilled at the prospect of a good fight. After a lifetime of constraining her gifts, the opportunity to flex some true magical muscle was like string dangling in front of a cat. She'd just set about braiding tiny crystals into a length of leather cord when the back door slid open.

"This is very nice." Thomas swaggered in, running his hand across the tile on the wall. "Spanish right?" He perched on a stool across from the kitchen table where she worked. "Conquistadors were my favorite."

The German Shepherd approached from under the table and bumped her knee with his nose.

Her heart thumped in her chest, but she lifted her chin and kept her voice steady. "I didn't invite you in here." She took a peanut butter cookie from a jar near the stove and fed it to the dog.

"I'm not a vampire, darling. I go wherever I want." He snapped his fingers and the dog moved to stand guard by the door.

Thomas held his hand out for a cookie, but she put the lid on the jar and returned to her work. The candle she lit earlier inched across the table in her direction while she braided the cord.

He seized it up and blew it out. "Show some respect. I'm here to chat with my eldest daughter. Do you know how special that makes you? With Brona gone, you're now the matriarch of what will be the mightiest dynasty ever."

She yawned.

"By the way, did you know that your mother was a powerful witch?"

Laura raised an eyebrow but said nothing.

"It's true, but your grandmother ruined everything. Brona didn't want any part of it because magic scared her to death. I can see why since Fiona beat that girl every time one of her spells failed."

"You're a liar."

He rolled his head around. "You see how the circle of abuse goes on and on?" He put a hand to his heart. "Personally, I think we should nurture our children's talents and desires, but I could be in the minority."

His story rolled her stomach. "Get out. Now."

"It's a lot to digest, I know. Let me ask you another question. Did you know Chuparosa was built on a ley line?"

"Everyone knows that."

"Yes, but they think it's all fairies and butterflies. Myself, I don't mess with the fairies. It was surprising to learn that you mess around with banshees of all things."

"Yeah, well they messed with us first, so we do what we can to get by."

"There are so many other beings on that Side-a veritable host of powers to draw from."

She stretched out the bracelet and began attaching a magnetic clasp. "Tell me, *Papa,* if we're so mighty, why do you need all those other powers? What do you want an army for?"

"I don't want a war, sweetie. I want to start over, but I have to fight for the chance." He gave his eyes a dramatic roll to the ceiling. "The first humans were given free will and then imprisoned in ignorance. It was so unfair, and they were insatiable for knowledge. We taught them magic and medicine."

"And weapons and war," she added.

He shrugged and continued, "We improved their race with our children. Why hide all of the knowledge they were literally designed to use?"

She paused. Her whole life had been spent defending her existence against the followers of the creator Thomas spoke of. Those that would sooner see her burn to death than use the power she was born with.

He leaned over the counter and batted his lashes at her. "I know you're angry about this too, my little abomination. I just want to create a safe space for our kind and for true free will to flourish."

"Raping witches and enslaving the Other Side hardly sounds like free will." Her eyes travelled to the door. "Speaking of which, what are you doing to that dog?"

"Your mother agreed, quite enthusiastically, to our terms. She wanted a normal life, and I gave her one.

"You make me sick."

He wound a strand of leather cord through his fingers. "You did nothing wrong, Laura. All this power runs in your veins but you'll never get in. You'll never see it. You are one of Heaven's lost. Lost for nothing more than a lack of foresight. Heaven's lost soldiers, lost worshipers, lost…defenders."

"You were there, but you left."

She thought she caught a flash of sorrow in his eyes, but it was gone in an instant. "I had to go where I was welcome."

She traced her finger across the scars on his wrist. "How'd that work out for you?"

He pushed her hand away. "Grow up, darling. This war has been raging for thousands of years, but it has nothing to do with good and evil. We can't go back home, but we don't have to stay where we are. You have a genetic technicality that makes you part of the fight, whether you like it or not. You can be a general, or you can be a drone, but you better not make yourself my enemy. Especially since I'm giving you the choice, a much more informed choice, by the way, than I had."


Laura was putting the finishing touches on her shield bracelets when Sarah and Audi walked in. The skin under Audi's eyes was still swollen and purple, but she had plenty of energy. So did Sarah for that matter.

"What's up with you? Your cheeks are damn near rosy."

Sarah flopped onto the couch. "It turns out demon fighting is a huge turn on for Rueben."

"Gak-Mom!"

Laura high-fived her and sat cross-legged on the coffee table. "I have more inconceivable news. Did you know mom was a witch?"

"You said bitch wrong."

"Thomas just left, and you won't believe this…"

"Thomas was here?" Audi turned in frantic circles. "Did you cleanse?"

She went to the cupboard where Laura kept dried sage from her garden, piled it in a dish, and lit the entire thing with a match.

"Anyway, he isn't working with the Other Side, he's controlling Adira and her attendants. That's why she didn't slash me into hamburger that day. She couldn't."

Sarah steepled her fingers and rested them against her chin. "She's probably pretty pissed about that, too. Good, her anger will make it easier."

She had a devious gleam in her eyes-a gleam Laura hadn't seen in a long time-and she eyed her suspiciously. "Make what easier?"

"I have a plan."

They all jumped as Daniel pushed open the front door and stood in front of them with his hands on his hips.

Laura took a marker from a drawer in the coffee table and handed it to Audi. "Make me a sign that says: 'No Angels Allowed.'"

"What do you think you're doing? Absorbing that demon was reckless."

Sarah stood in front of him defiantly. "It was part of us once, so we took it back."

Daniel covered his face with his hands and said, "It's not like you lost a shoe."

Audi pulled out the jar of cookies and said to Laura, "These aren't oatmeal raisin, are they?"

He followed the sisters to the kitchen. "It was irresponsible."

Sarah took the jar from Audi. "Have a cookie. You eat, don't you?"

"Of course, I eat." It had been decades since he'd enjoyed a cookie though. He took a bite and paused, closing his eyes to appreciate it. "This is scrumptious."

Laura pursed her lips, "If you're going to kill us, please do it now. Otherwise listen up, because Thomas is tired of Hell. He wants to build a whole new kingdom full of all the things that should not be. A safe space for us in-between types that you hate so much."

She tapped her chin and looked thoughtfully into his eyes. "If I'm being honest Daniel, I don't think it's the worst idea ever. But, after all that time down there, he's completely unhinged. We have to stop him, and we have to do it soon."

Daniel took another cookie. "I don't hate you." He moved toward her, but she backed away, so he finished the cookie, dusted off his hands and held them out to her. "Please, it won't be the same this time."

"Laura, no." Sarah stepped between them.

Daniel realized, too late of course, that it had been unwise to threaten them during their first meeting. He did not expect his actions to strengthen their resolve and close their ranks against him. He'd planned to frighten to them into his service, but they had no use for him or their long-absent father, angels or not. He wondered with amusement if Thomas had been just as surprised. He could not control their actions, but they would indeed make formidable Defenses if he could gain their trust.

He stepped around Sarah and once again extended his hands. Laura reached out with no small amount of trepidation until they were almost touching.

Sarah grimaced, "Don't you hurt her."

Laura took a small step forward and braced herself as she rested her hands in his. She could feel…nothing. She felt less than she would shaking a stranger's hand, which is how she knew it wasn't right.

"Everything gives off energy so where is yours? Does this mean you can decide how it feels to someone you touch?"

He nodded, and she cast Sarah a knowing glance. Assuming Thomas could do the same, they'd just learned something incredibly useful.

"You are very much like Thomas," he said.

When Laura blanched, he added, "I only meant that you share a misinterpretation about your origins."

Sarah sniffed, "The phrase you're looking for is generational trauma".

## Chapter Twenty

When Sebastian left Laura's house, he headed to Isaac's for a beer, a burger, and some time to think, but Dirk Schmidt waved him down as he walked through the restaurant.

"Sheriff, you may want to do something about that." Bash followed Dirk's gaze to the long bar in the back where Drew sat, obviously drunk. "It's not a good look for the church."

A year earlier, when Dirk's wife left him, he got drunk himself and drove his car into a canal. Bash arrested him for driving under the influence, but Andrew Clarke sat in the jail cell all night while Dirk had a mental breakdown over the incident. Drew arranged treatment for Dirk and counseling for the whole family. Bash couldn't believe that the bastard had the nerve to judge anyone, let alone Drew.

He loomed over Dirk. "What did you say?"

"We're just concerned," Dirk muttered, and quickly sat down.

Bash turned his back on the Schmidts and took in the scene. Drew was not quite upright on a stool at the end of the bar with several empty shot glasses in front of him. Isaac had been bartending, which he rarely did in those days, so he must have felt like Drew needed a babysitter. His relief when he saw Bash was evident. The whole place hushed, awaiting Bash's next move but he surprised them all and took a seat next to Drew at the bar.

"I'll have one of these," he said, picking up one of Drew's shot glasses.

Isaac cleared the empties. "Really?"

"Sure, why not?" Isaac poured the shot and Bash gave it a sniff. *Why was it always tequila?*

Drew looked around the bar and put his head down, "I feel so stupid."

Bash downed his shot, made a face and said, "Nobody in this place has any room to talk."

"I don't mean them."

"I know." When Isaac turned up the music to keep people out of their business, Bash added, "We don't get to decide who we have feelings for. Sometimes it's just bad luck."

He stood up and put a couple of twenties on the bar. "Will this cover it?"

Isaac pushed the money back and said, "Don't be an asshole."

Bash gave him his thanks, and they hoisted Drew to his feet.

Out back Isaac chuckled, "He's gonna puke in your truck," but his tone sobered once Drew was situated. "Look man, I don't know what's happening, but I can feel that something's not right in this town. If I can help, you better tell me."

Bash clapped a hand on his shoulder. "I'm gonna go deal with this." He thumbed back at Drew, who was leaning forward with his head on the dash. "Then I'll be in touch."


They sat in Drew's driveway for several minutes while Bash figured out the logistics of their upcoming adventure.

"Where are your keys?"

Drew stared at him for a second and then bounced his head against the window.

"That's great," Bash grumbled and shoved his hand in Drew's pocket.

Inside, he dropped Drew on the couch and did a walkthrough. In the main bathroom, he whisked open the shower curtain and was startled nearly out of his shoes when Drew's tabby cat leapt from the tub and scrambled out of the room.

"Holy crap!"

Back in the living room, the cat hissed at him from her perch atop the scratching post.

"Relax, I'm not gonna hurt your dad." He flipped up the medallion hanging from her collar and read her name. "Daphne? Jesus," he sighed. "Okay, Miss Daphne, we've got to get him to the back."

Daphne's contribution to the exercise was to run a zigzag pattern between their feet but Bash managed to get Drew in front of the toilet just in time for him to hit his knees and heave.

After several minutes, Drew tried to stand, but Bash worried he would crack his skull if he fell in that cramped space, so he pushed his head over the side of the tub and turned on the shower.

As the cold water hit the back of Drew's neck, Bash mused with genuine sympathy, "That was only round one buddy," and pulled out his phone.

When Rhonda answered, he blurted, "What have you got for a hangover? A bad one."

"Sebastian, you know better, you're way too old to be drinking that much."

"It's not for me, woman."

Drew groaned loudly as he hurled again, and the wretched sound set her skin tingling with alarm.

"What's going on?"

"Andrew Clarke is throwing up his soul, and I do *not* want to bring Laura over here right now. Rhonda, can you help me? Please?"

"Oh, boy. You're at his house? I'll be right there."

He wrangled Drew over the side of the tub again and then leaned against the doorframe to catch his breath.

Twenty minutes later, Rhonda stood in the doorway of Drew's bathroom trying to process the scene in front of her without laughing. The shower was on, Drew was face down on the bathmat, and Bash was seated on the floor with his back propped against the cabinet. Both men were soaking wet, and Daphne sat in judgment from the sink.

"I'm sure you boys will think this is funny in a few years." She handed Bash a towel. "Let's get him out of here."

His head lolled, but Drew was able to sit up on the side of the bed. She took a small jar out of her bag and put it to his lips, but he sniffed at it and pushed her hand away, so Bash grabbed his nose. When Drew's mouth opened, she poured in the contents of the jar and then he fell over on the bed with a loud moan and curled himself up in the fetal position.

"What was in that?"

She blinked at him. "Don't ask questions you don't want the answers to, Sheriff."

"Oh, great."

Drew's wet clothes were soaking into the mattress, so Rhonda searched through his dresser for a pair of sweatpants and a t-shirt.

Bash shook his head. "No. Absolutely not."

"He can't stay like that, he'll catch pneumonia."

"Aw, hell."

When they pulled off his shirt, Rhonda put a hand to her mouth and gasped, "Oh, my word."

Bash set his jaw and snatched Drew's belt from the bed. It was a perfect fit in the deep scars on Drew's back. "A man's belt." He said and threw it on the floor with disgust. "These marks are old, someone did this to him when he was a boy."

When they got him changed and settled on the couch, Bash ran his hand along Daphne's back and said, "I can't thank you enough, Rhonda. I'll stay here and keep an eye on him."

She handed him a large bottle of what was ostensibly a sports drink, though the liquid was a color he'd never seen before.

"You're a good man, Sebastian."

"No, but he is, and I don't want him choking to death by himself."

She gave him a long hug. "You don't fool me, honey. I'll be back in the morning."

Bash fumbled around the kitchen looking for caffeine and learned that, mercifully, Drew had a normal coffee machine. After brewing a full pot, he took the Encyclopedia of Demons off the table, threw a towel over Drew's leather chair, and he and Daphne sat down to read.

Soon he began to fidget and stood up to stretch. Uncomfortable in his wet clothes and anxious from the demon book, he took a more extended walking tour of Drew's house. It was of Spanish Colonial design like Laura's, though the preacher lacked her sense of style. Laura and Bash were avid readers, but their book collections could not compare with Drew's. Nearly every wall in the house was lined with shelves loaded two deep with volumes.

Drew's collection included what you would expect to find in a Christian preacher's house and there were other religious texts as well, some about faiths Bash had never heard of. He was relieved to learn that along with philosophy and history, there was plenty of popular culture. He smiled to himself when he noticed that they shared a fondness for Elmore Leonard.

Clearly Daphne ran the place, as evidenced by the scattered toys and the multilevel cat condo set up in front of a primary window in the living room. She followed Bash to the kitchen and sat glaring next to her empty bowl.

"Alright, alright." He looked around for the food, then scooped some from a large plastic bin into her dish.

On the table, he noticed a thick book that was open and turned upside down with a notepad next to it. Drew had been scribbling furiously about something he found inside, and Bash didn't nose through the other man's notes but he picked up the book and observed where he had highlighted a particular sentence:

*...and the angels would rely on certain Defenses- humans and other creatures who could be trusted in the battle for the Earth...*

He did not like the implications of that and felt ashamed for mocking the man's research earlier. Laura was right. Andrew was helping them, and they were incredibly lucky to have him.

Sometime before dawn, Drew jerked awake with his throat on fire and an ache throughout his entire body. Bash helped him sit up and gave him the sports drink.

"Sip it slow," he cautioned.

A fresh wave of agony surged through Drew's body as shame took hold. He placed the drink on the floor and put his head in his hands.

"I don't even know what to say to you right now. What you did for me…"

Bash ignored him and returned to the reading chair. "How the hell does an electrician preacher land in Chuparosa?"

Drew hiccuped. "I left Riverside in…"

"Ugh, don't tell me you're from California."

"Yep, but I won't bore you with the details."

Bash pointed to the bottle on the floor. "Drink some of that. The Theology degree hanging in your room is dated 1994. Why don't you start there?"

Drew took a sip, grimaced and sat back. "When you're the most disappointing son, there are three disappointments in total, of serious and I mean *serious* believers, you grow up thinking that a career in the church will," he smirked knowingly to himself, "somehow validate your existence."

Bash bit the inside of his cheek. *Belt mystery solved.* "Is there any money in that?"

"Nope. Especially at the lowest levels. I started working as an electrician's apprentice after college and ended up as a volunteer minister at my church. I did it for years. I made it to journeyman, became more involved at church, found a wife, and lost a wife. I was just living."

"What made you leave?"

Drew shifted uncomfortably on the couch. "The church asked me to quit when I got divorced." His head began to throb, and he took another sip.

"No kids?" Bash pressed.

"Ha. No." Drew's short laugh could not hide his bitterness. "Turns out it's me, I can't have kids. I was ready to adopt a houseful though. I thought that might be my real calling, but she wanted her own. When she finally did get pregnant, she left me for him."

"Wow."

"Anyway, I had to get out of there. I put my house up for sale and thought I could find work in Phoenix but the 4Runner overheated right outside of Chuparosa." He allowed himself a crooked smile as the memory took on a more pleasant feel. "It was so damn hot that day and I was standing there with a dead phone, pissed off, and hating my life when Laura and Brian pulled over next to me."

Bash's chest tightened at the thought of Laura stopping for a random stranger on the side of the highway, but he reminded himself she wouldn't have done it if it didn't feel right.

"Brian took her .38 out of the glove box and threatened to shoot me if I did anything weird but he called Arley's Service Station for a tow. Laura said she'd give me a ride to town but swore she would tase me if I touched her."

Bash threw his head back and laughed, "God, I love that woman."

"Well, she's allergic to church so I didn't see her very often after that. You know the rest. Sarah shows up almost every Sunday by herself. We became friends and…"

Drew stumbled to the coffee pot, poured a cup, took a sip, and waited for his stomach to react.

"You know, the moral implications of my feelings are horrific enough but it's excruciating to watch her beg for scraps of his attention when I would build my whole world around her."

Bash stood and poured himself another cup of coffee. "Rueben's all right, he just forgot what matters. I'm standing here guilty of that myself."

"No. You were just mixed up. He checked out a long time ago."

"Listen, be careful what you wish for. You've got to be ready for how it's gonna work."

Drew put the coffee cup to his forehead. "What are you talking about? If she looked at me just once the way Laura looks at you, I would die a happy man."

Bash swallowed hard. "The reality of loving a woman like that is that she doesn't need you for anything. You can't make her stop and you can't protect her. Call me a toxic caveman if you want to but I had a hard time with that. I mean, what was I even bringing to the table?"

Drew hadn't considered it that way. It was true that in all of his fantasies, he was rescuing Sarah. But from what, exactly? A marriage she could leave on her own if she wanted to? A demon she created herself?

Bash rubbed at the long-ignored stubble along his jaw. *Was Laura serious about loving a beard?* "Turns out, what I bring to the table is me. We're partners and she loves me, the poor thing. As for Rueben, it's more complicated when you get married that young." He stumbled over the words in his next sentence. "It can be like-like watching a slow death."

Drew sensed that the stalwart sheriff had his own horror stories to tell, but the coffee churned in his stomach, so he decided to pursue them at another time.

Bash opened the refrigerator and pushed around some condiments. Like most bachelors, Drew shopped at 'take out.' "My guess is," he said, closing the door, "having Audi was a hail Mary that kept them going until now, but she's grown and they're right back where they started, only worse. He will either get his shit together or she'll leave him, but you can't wait around being miserable."

Drew bowed his head, "I know...I know."

Just then, Rhonda burst in with an armful of bags.

Bash gave her a look. "I know I locked that door."

"I stole his keys." She tossed them on the kitchen table and took out two breakfast burritos wrapped in aluminum foil. Bash tore into one and kissed the top of her head while Drew backed away as she pulled out another small jar and put it down in front of him.

"Your shift is over, sweetie," she said to Bash. "Go home and get some sleep."

He took another bite of his burrito, paused at the door, and turned to Drew. "Those people in California? It's their loss."

## Chapter Twenty-One

Brian was having what they called an 'awakened practice' that afternoon. Often, some subtle bit of coaching would resonate out of the blue, resulting in a better time. Just as often, one's 'mere mortal' status could be hammered home in spectacular fashion.

On that day, Brian was awakened to the understanding that he could not finish a lab experiment at two in the morning and expect to perform well in the pool.

The coach nailed him hard for a lazy butterfly, so he had to spend twenty minutes doing breaststroke, which he hated. Frustrated and embarrassed, he took an extra-long cool down while his teammates packed up and the lifeguards reeled in the lane lines.

From the bleachers, Thomas watched his grandson's body skim across the water in an effortless backstroke that was slow and measured to release the tension in his overworked muscles. He would have cheerfully throttled the coach because lazy or not, Thomas observed that Brian's butterfly was one of the team's best. But he knew competition ranked high in the human pantheon of gods, and Brian seemed to accept his punishment without question.

The lifeguards finished locking up the equipment and waved Brian goodbye. He'd noticed Thomas in the bleachers a few hours earlier and took his time gathering his things. His mother warned him about the true identity of the man from the bar, but she'd convinced herself that Brian's far away location and lack of powers assured that Thomas was uninterested in him.

According to Audi, the angel's primary objectives were down in the valley, but no one had observed how much more transpired during their brief interaction. The detestable sensation of Thomas slithering through his mind had suffused his thoughts since the St. Patrick's Day party, so Brian was not surprised when he stepped on the deck and handed him a towel.

"Hello, Brian."

He ignored the towel and busied himself with his gear. "I wondered when you would show up here."

"I wasn't sure if your mother told you about me."

Brian pulled on his sweatpants. "She keeps me informed."

Thomas rocked back on his heels. "Ah, but you don't return the favor, do you? Tell me why you chose electrical engineering. Are you that eager to build better light bulbs or is there something else?"

"What do you want from me?"

"I want to get to know my grandson. I'm interested in what matters to you."

While his mother's courage ran through his veins, so did her impassioned temperament, and something

Laura told him about Drew shook his stoic resolve. "Then why did you kick the shit out of my friend?"

Thomas thrilled at inadvertently hitting such a nerve. "Oh, the preacher? I guess that makes sense. He's an electrician, so I suppose he has his uses. Or is it that he fills the father square in your life?"

"Leave him alone."

Thomas put his hands in his pockets and tapped the roll of lane lines with his boot. "What about Sebastian Scott, everyone's favorite cowboy?"

Brian narrowed his eyes. "Fuck Sebastian Scott."

Thomas laid a supportive hand on the young man's shoulder. "My sentiments exactly."

A familiar pulse of energy knotted itself in Brian's belly and he shoved him away. "I said what do you want from me?"

Thomas built a ball of electricity in his hands and casually tossed it to him. Brian deflected it up to the security cameras overhead causing them to spark and pop.

"I want to know why you never told your mother you could do that."

Brian recalled an afternoon at another pool where his seven-year-old self had first learned to play with the light. Back then Laura bought him swimming lessons at the five-foot deep Chuparosa community pool.

That community center had since been converted into a YMCA with an Olympic sized pool, solar powered cover, and bleachers for when the high school teams competed there. When Brian was little, the water was wide open to the elements and the insects, including the yellow jackets that plagued the swimmers every year.

A determined wasp had found its way to the beginning of his lesson that day, menacing the teenaged instructor and eliciting shrieks from the children who attempted to splash it away. Of course, it wasn't long before a little girl's scream could be heard above the commotion. Brian dangled his feet in the water as the adults attended to the angry red welt that grew on her forearm.

As the girl's cries grew more hysterical from the pain, Brian was overcome with an intense hatred for all stinging things, and it was a sentiment that he would carry throughout adulthood. To his horror, the wasp landed atop the water next to him and, for reasons he could not explain at the time, he floated his hand on the surface of the water next to it.

As it bobbed closer, he turned his palm up, and when it poised to attack him, a thread of green light radiated from his hand. The light trapped the creature as if it had flown into an electrical spider web, toasting it black and sinking it like a rock to the bottom of the pool.

Laura never hid her magical nature from her son or anyone else. She was proud of the things she could do but he knew she suffered because of them. Men didn't trust her, everyone gossiped about her, and her own mother despised her. Brian understood early on that he couldn't protect her from any of that, but he made the decision to protect her from himself.

It was perhaps Laura's and Sarah's suffering that influenced how Audi was trained to keep such tight control over her powers. He was under no such regulation as long as his abilities remained hidden from everyone but his cousin.

Unfortunately, the arrival of Thomas in their lives meant that he was sure to be exposed. He'd always known the day would come but had hoped to be well-launched into adulthood by then and thus able to reach his mother on her level, without groveling like a child.

He gave half an answer to the question, hoping Thomas didn't have full access to his thoughts. "I didn't want to be like Audi, I wanted to figure it out for myself."

"Aha," Thomas tapped his chin. "And you would rather be free to test your limits on your own."

"So what?"

"So, I need a favor along those lines."

Brian zipped his bag. "I'm not doing shit for you."

He grabbed the boy by the throat and raised him off the ground. "I'm getting sick and tired of that sentence. You audacious fetus, I could kill you right now."

Brian choked and clutched at Thomas' hands but looked him in the eyes and said, "Do it then."

Thomas found it interesting that Brian's generation had such a cavalier attitude toward death. Perhaps it was because on any given day, they were never sure they would make it home from high school alive. A useful inclination sometimes, annoying at others.

He knew that if he harmed her son, Laura would not rest until she found a way to burn down all of Hell. He was of the belief that would not be a bad thing in the long run. In fact, he vowed to encourage the endeavor in the future. For the time being though, he needed his whole family working together so he dropped the boy to the deck.

He straightened his jacket while Brian gasped for breath on the tile. "I'll tell you the truth, son, I'm not here to hurt anyone. Andrew Clarke is fine, by the way. I was just trying to make a point that day. You must understand that your mother is precious to me and, believe it or not, I think she may be coming around to my way of thinking."

Brian rubbed his throat. "You didn't spend much time with her, did you?"

"I know that you're thinking, 'what's in it for me?' I get that." He offered Brain a hand up.

"Wouldn't you like a place where you could be free to express yourself? Where people like you could grow their talents without judgment? What if you never again had to hide in the shadows, in Audi's shadow?"

Brian took his hand, ignoring the energy that raced through him as Thomas hauled him to his feet.

"There is no place like that."

Thomas smiled. "Chuparosa is the perfect place. I myself am tired of hiding out and I need a home base. Brian, I want that town and we could even have the job done by summer break. What do you say?"

* * *

Adira's two bobcats were waiting for them at the bottom of the canyon and when she caught sight of them, Audi shifted her backpack from one shoulder to the other, wishing she'd packed a joint.

"It looks like the Bobs are here to block the way."

Sarah unzipped a pouch in Audi's pack and pulled out a jar. "Tell her we know what he did."

Audi put the offering, a bowl of wildflower honey, on the ground in front of the cats. The Bobs padded in circles around them, ignoring the dish and one of them swiped lightly at Sarah's calf.

Audi stomped her foot and shouted, "Hey!"

The Bob pressed into its hind limbs, ready to pounce so Sarah plucked the dish from the ground and poured the honey in the sand. "Fine. Have fun when Thomas comes for you."

Adira's roar echoed through the canyon and her voice pierced their minds. "How dare you? If I could, I would kill you now for your insults."

Sarah wasted no time. "I know, but how is he doing it, Adira? How is he controlling you like this?"

The mountain lion sprang from above and paced in front of them, swishing her tail in annoyance. Sarah reached in Audi's pack again and held out Adira's geode to show it had been restored. "Let me make things right."

Adira flattened her ears and instructed one of the Bobs to take the geode away. He locked it between his jaws and scurried into the portal.

"You recovered your lost power?"

Audi sat cross-legged in the sand in front of the remaining bobcat, holding out her hand. He would either bite her or let her pet him and at that point she didn't care which.

"Sometimes, my mom is kind of awesome."

"Adira, what has that man, that angel, done to you?"

She seethed at Bob, hissing and spitting with frustration. "He enslaved them first, the fools." Then she held up a scarred paw to show where she'd been slashed. "I bargained with him for their release, but he betrayed us."

It was as Sarah suspected. "I can break the bargain for you."

"Stupid witch. It is blood magic, his blood."

Sarah pulled a pocketknife from her jeans and slid the blade across the palm of her hand. "Guess what? A whole lot of his blood runs through me."

Adira tossed her head in disgust. She was unconvinced that Sarah could break the spell but told them what she knew. "He comes and goes through a circle of sand, but only when the moon is high. He brings creatures with him that I've never seen before. They are not from my realm."

"We believe he's most powerful at night and I'm pretty sure he's got demons working for him too." Sarah motioned to Audi, who took several bags of pink salt from her pack and got to work on a giant circle in the sand outside the mountain lion's portal.

"If you fail, I will shred the skin from your body," Adira threatened.

"If I fail, that will be preferable to anything else that awaits me."

## Chapter Twenty-Two

"Why are you wet?"

Sebastian tossed his hat on Laura's table and plopped in a chair. "It's not as bad as it was. I spent the night at Drew's place."

About forty legitimate questions cycled through her mind, but she sat on his lap and suppressed a smile, teasing, "Is he a better kisser than me?"

He gave her a squeeze. "That's cute. But unlike you, he would have much better taste in men. It's not a big deal. He got a little too drunk and needed a babysitter."

She lowered her eyelids. "Is he sad because he's in love with my sister?"

He twirled a lock of her hair between his fingers. "I should have known you'd figure that out."

"He's not exactly Mr. Mysterious, but it was just a hunch until now. I don't think Sarah has a clue; she's focused on the fact that our lives are falling apart. Is he alright?"

"Other than hating himself and nursing one hell of a hangover, he's fine."

Laura considered Andrew to be the best of them. If he hated himself, she thought she should have walked into traffic a long time ago. Her thoughts were interrupted when Bash took notice of a large black spot burned in the countertop.

"What have you been doing?"

She'd been attempting to coat her fingernails with phosphorus paper in a sort of weaponized manicure. The first two experiments resulted in small and not-so-small failures, so she explained that he'd arrived right before her third attempt.

He flipped her hand over in his. "What if you just did the tips?"

If she didn't get some more sleep, little oversights like that would soon become fatal. "Yes, of course. Like a French manicure. I'm so stupid."

He rubbed his eyes. "Baby, I don't know what that means." He was so tired that she might as well have been *speaking* French.

She wiggled against him. "It doesn't matter, I should have thought of it myself, but you just saved the day."

He had no idea how, but he would take the win.

"Oh, yeah, this too." She set a shield bracelet in front of him. "Put this on, so I can make sure it fits. It's not perfect, but it will give you some extra protection out there."

He curled his lip and pushed at the black obsidian stones.

He tugged on her arm as she headed to for the bedroom for more nail supplies, and said, "Grab some things for later."

"Why?"

"Because we need to sleep, and you're gonna be in

my bed tonight."

The look she gave him was defiant, but only briefly before she winked and dropped the bracelet in his hand. "Put. It. On."

The invisible shield pulsed against his body as the magnets closed around his wrist and he tugged at her again. "Baby, do you have another one of these?"

In her bedroom, Audi alternately stared down at the textbook on her desk and out the window, absently tapping a pen on her chin, unable to focus clearly on anything since the incident with Bob Mercer. As the dust kicked up outside, she felt like her brain was full of those tiny grains of sand whipping chaotically through the air. She knew she needed help, but her first meeting with a mental health professional was sure to be a disaster.

"It all started with clairvoyant visions when I was eleven. And we recently found out that my grandfather is a fallen angel." She confessed to the mirror, giggling at the horrified look on her imaginary therapist.

Mercer was alive, but they were keeping him at Phoenix General Hospital and Sheriff Ruiz said he had no memory of what happened. The doctors assumed it was amnesia or some other brain injury from the crash. Since the crime was so out of character for him, they even considered that he may have a brain tumor. Her family knew better though.

Aunt Laura said Thomas had orchestrated the whole thing, which was somehow worse in Audi's mind than a random pervert kidnapping. Thomas scared the shit out of her. If he could drop a strong man like Pastor

Clarke and control those deadly animals there was no knowing how truly dangerous he was.

She shuddered and considered sending Noah a cute study selfie as a distraction. She flipped her phone camera to front facing but thought better of it after another look at her image. There were still dark purple bruises under her eyes and the lacerations across her neck were scabbing over. *Gross. I look more like a case study than a cutie.* She thought about sending him something sexy from the neck down but lost her courage.

She tried to meditate but saw Bob Mercer's maniacal face in the review mirror every time she closed her eyes. After four or five deep breaths, the image of her cousin floated through her mind and she picked up her phone again.

When the Skyrim theme rang out, she blurted, "Hey, do you get Olivia's nudes?"

"Nah."

"Hmmm. Okay."

"I heard Mercer's gonna live. What about you?"

"Unclear at this time."

"So, I got a visit from Grandpa."

She grabbed a pillow from her bed and clutched it to her chest. "Brian, be careful. You don't understand what he's capable of."

"He knows about me."

"Oh, no," she whispered.

"Audi, he had some good ideas if you think about it. Wouldn't you like to have a safe place to use your power? Some place where we can live with all the others like us? With instant acceptance?"

"That place is called Chuparosa, Brian."

"Yeah, like those people who accept Mom and Aunt

Sarah? No thanks. And I mean *all* of the others. Thomas wants to…"

"Thomas is enslaving all of the others. Do you think he won't do that to us too? He'll turn our home into a prison."

"Have you told Noah about what you can do? How did he react?"

She rolled her eyes. "He wants to help everyone, human or not. Noah won't be allowed in Thomas' world. I know you don't like Sheriff Scott, but your mom sure does. He won't be allowed in either. And Pastor Clarke? Thomas really hates him."

Brian was quiet, so she pressed him further. "You've got to tell Laura what you can do. It's time."


Bash and Laura fell into the entryway of his house, punch drunk from exhaustion and grinding on each other like teenagers. Stress and fear fueled their intense need to be as close as possible.

The lock had barely clicked when she knelt and unbuttoned his jeans. He buried his hands in her hair as she took him into her mouth. His head fell back, and he murmured, "Oh, my God, Laura."

He pulled her up and kissed her hard while sliding his hands under her dress. He'd slid her panties off in his truck on the way over, so he pushed into her with ease, curling his arm under her knee and driving her back against the door.

His rough hunger thrilled her. After all they'd been through, she was desperate to lose herself under the weight of him, and he felt so good. As the grip slid from his self-control, he begged, "Come for me, baby," and she went right over the edge, biting into his shoulder as her body shuddered against his.

"God, damn," he groaned as the door rattled in protest against the force of his final thrusts. He rested his head on her collarbone, and she wrapped him in her arms as they stood there for several moments, trembling and catching their breath. Finally, he led her to the bedroom where they collapsed in a deep sleep.

Late the next morning, she leaned against the refrigerator scrolling her phone and wearing only Sebastian's t-shirt while he fixed their breakfast of bagels, bacon, and coffee.

Daniel pushed open the backdoor and Bash moved in front of Laura with his fists raised. "Get out of my house!"

Daniel was unmoved by his outrage. "It's not like I can call in advance."

"You can fucking knock."

"I'll have Audi make you a sign," Laura said. She rubbed Bash's back and made her way to the bedroom, adding over her shoulder, "It's a good thing he didn't show up last night."

Daniel raised an eyebrow and selected a bagel from the paper bag on Bash's counter. He spread on some cream cheese and took a bite from one half. "You need to be ready to act," he said with his mouthful, "today."

Bash mentally shifted gears. "Everyone is waiting for my call."

"Make it. Thomas is on the move."

Laura returned having added a pair of running shorts to her outfit. She swiped the other half of

Daniel's bagel and took a bite. "Sarah says the Other Side is vibrating with fear, the veil over their portal is paper thin right now."

"He's harnessed the power of their portal to construct a gate. I believe he intends to use it to bring things with him to Hell."

Bash sipped his coffee and rubbed his forehead. "Hell needs supplies?"

Laura licked some cream cheese off her finger and without looking up said, "He means *things* like me."

Daniel nodded. "It makes sense. You'll probably survive the journey, and he could keep you there until you agreed to help him."

Bash was incredulous, looking from Laura to Daniel and back again. "He's not taking you anywhere."

"He already controls the guardians of the Other Side and I'm sure he plans to combine their power with hers."

"Did you not hear what I said? He's not taking her anywhere. He's not doing any more damage. We'll stop him, all of us, and that includes you."

Bash abandoned his coffee and took out a beer, ignoring Daniel's stern look.

"Yep, it's ten o'clock on a Tuesday and I'm sitting here with a witch, talking to an angel about fighting a demon." He put the bottle to his lips and gave Daniel the middle finger.

Bash had several boxes of ammunition piled on the kitchen counter that caught the angel's attention. "Your bullets won't work on everything he sends after you."

Bash made a face. "Let's not borrow trouble. Whatever he sends, we'll have to make do."

Daniel arranged the boxes in a single layer, then

flattened his hands on the counter. A pulse of white light flowed across the granite and was absorbed by the ammo. "I can't promise I'll be able to provide the kind of help you want, Sebastian. But that should give you an edge."

Bash was not willing to give Daniel the impression that he was grateful. Instead, he finished his beer and pulled out his phone. "I'm calling the others."

Laura took a wooden spoon from a canister by the stove and used it to push the ammo boxes from the counter's edge. "No offense, but I still don't want to get too close to anything you've had your hands on."

Daniel restacked the boxes. "You're part of my family, Laura."

"But you will punish me if I don't play by your rules. I guess it's comforting to know the dynamics in Heaven aren't that different than they are here on earth."

For a moment he appeared sad, but his eyes recovered their serenity and he said, "Remember that he's most powerful in the hours just before midnight and the veil will be at its thinnest right before dawn. Your window is very small."

She took another bite of his bagel. "Of course it is."

## Chapter Twenty-Three

As the sun set over the mountains, Bash and Drew met Rueben, Chuck, and Isaac near Adira's portal at the bottom of Ford Canyon. Chuck's left arm hung in a sling, but his right fingers tapped on the pistol holstered at his hip.

Rueben and Isaac hoisted shotguns to their shoulders, scanning the area and then turning to Bash, asked, "Where do you want us?"

Bash gestured to the horizon. "Get up on that ridge and put down whatever he sends after us." He gave them each two boxes of Daniel's reinforced shells, adding, "Use these."

They filled the shotgun chambers and dumped the rest of the shells in the pockets of their cargo pants while Bash handed Chuck three preloaded magazines.

He dug in his shirt pocket for the second bracelet Laura made and tossed it to Drew. "Put that on."

Drew clapped it to his wrist and his head snapped back in astonishment as the force of Laura's shield settled around his body.

Chuck grinned. "Does this mean you two are going steady?"

Bash spun the cylinder on his revolver. "If you want, I'll shoot you first."


Bash found Laura by the Jeep and cupped her face in his hands. "You know, when you said you had daddy issues, I had no idea what you meant."

She rested her head on his chest. "Just tell me we can pull this off."

He tugged on the zipper of her top. "Here's another crystal for you." He'd picked up the glowing black stone the day they met Daniel. An energy surge lifted her shoulders as he dropped it into her sports bra, zipped up the top and kissed her lips. "We will help *you* pull it off."


When the others headed to the ridge, Drew gave Audi a handful of metal tent spikes. She scanned the ground for the pink salt circle she'd made the day before, then pulled a hammer from her back pocket.

Adira paced inside the circle sniffing impatiently at Sarah, who was securing two taper candles connected with several inches of thick twine to the top of a flat rock. To her dismay, the banshee had chosen that afternoon to start wailing, quashing what meager confidence she'd woken up with.

"Can't you do anything about that?"

Adira shook her head. "To forfeit such a gift is madness."

Though she couldn't be certain who the wailing was for, they all knew that Laura had only the slightest chance of defeating Thomas. With trembling hands, she prepped the last of the materials that could shift her sister's fate. *The one time I decide to work my own spell.*

She had told no one but Drew about the banshee that day. He pulled a bandana from his pocket and wiped at the sweat on her forehead while she worked and tried to reassure her. "Laura is so much stronger than the banshees think."

His words did provide some hope. Though the banshees had never been wrong, it was true that one of Laura's greatest powers was that of surprise.

When Sarah's preparations were complete, she ran a knife over her forearm, letting droplets of blood coat one of the candles.

Adira rested one of her paws on Drew's knee and ordered, "Do it quickly, Preacher."

He sliced a knife through the pad and squeezed a few drops of her blood on the other candle. In theory, as the blood coated twine burned away, so would Thomas' hold over Adira and her minions. She was still not convinced it would work and hissed at them as she limped away to lick her wound.

Drew peeled opened a large bandage and secured it to Sarah's arm. They watched the big cat for a while and then Sarah knelt over her spell with some final words of caution for him. "Remember, they have to do what Thomas tells them to. They're not acting of their own free will, so don't hurt them."

The Bobs stalked toward Bash and Drew, who pulled their guns and put their backs together as outside the circle, a thick cloud of dust rolled up the wash.

"Adira said that's his gate," Sarah warned.

Through the haze, Thomas stepped out with the ever-present German Shepherd at his side and Laura flicked her nails and pulled the flames into her palm.


Up on the ridge, Isaac was the first to notice the creatures as they emerged from the darkness.

"Head's up." He told the others.

"Shit." Rueben counted six massive, sand-colored lizard-like beings slinking across the ground toward the canyon with thick, long tails and sharp horns. "What in the hell is that?"

"You've got me." When Chuck caught sight of Thomas in the dust cloud below, he used his good hand to rack the pistol slide against his belt. "They've got enough problems down there so whatever those things are, keep them up here." He fired on one of the creatures, hitting it in the back of the head. The head exploded into a fine mist of blood and ash while its body writhed on the ground.

Rueben took a shell out of his pocket and held it up. "Did Bash say what he loaded these things with?"

The other creatures all turned their heads at once, glaring with glowing green eyes.

Isaac shook his head. "Nope, but I'd say we got their attention."


Down below, Thomas filled his hands with blue knots of electricity. "I read somewhere that the oldest daughter shares many characteristics with her father.

I'm no psychologist, but I think that must be why we fight."

Laura's flame ballooned. "We fight because you're insane and," she said with cold smile, "I hate you."

Sebastian's chest heaved with worry. "Baby, please don't antagonize him."

Drew leaned into his friend's back, "Focus, man." The Bobs stood near Adira, crouched forward and flicking their stubby tails, ready to lunge.

Several shots were fired from the ridge and as they looked up, the Bobs took advantage and pounced, but when the men raised their arms in defense, the bobcats bounced off the power in Laura's shields.


Back on the ridge, Rueben shot at something new as it dropped in front of them from the trees.

"I guess we've got goblins now too, dammit."

As a dozen of the gangly creatures advanced on them, Chuck reminded the others, "Just don't let the demons get away."

"Not a problem!" Isaac was on the ground about a hundred feet away, his empty shotgun lying beside him as one of the demons cornered him against a large boulder. It snapped its jaws and drool smoked and sizzled as it dripped on the ground between his legs.

Chuck fired but missed. Even so, he'd provided Isaac with valuable seconds as the demon turned its head toward the distraction. He jumped up and away as Chuck fired again, that time hitting it square in the chest. The demon howled with outrage as Daniel's power coursed through its body with agonizing precision, tearing it apart all the way to its tail.

Isaac pulled five shells out of his pocket and jammed them in the chamber. He knew there were two demons left, but scanning the area, he could see only goblins.

"Oh, no."

Something screeched from behind them, and Bash swung around to shoot a goblin that hovered outside the salt circle. "There must be too many for them to handle up there."

Drew grabbed Bash's arm to draw his attention to a demon lashing its tail and creeping up behind Laura. "Where did that thing come from?"

They were not close enough for Bash to take a shot, so he gave Drew a nod and left the circle, running toward the creature and hoping to get close enough before Thomas saw him coming. He had no such luck as the demon tipped its head and gored Laura's calf with its horn.

She swore as her leg buckled and threw a stream of fire at the beast who shook it off as if it were a breeze.

Bash yelled, "Laura!" and Thomas whirled on him with a pulse of lightning. It barely permeated Laura's shield, but it was enough to throw him on his back.

The demon abandoned Laura to stalk Bash, who sat up and fired three rounds into it, dead center. The demon thrummed and glowed white from its pores and Bash scrambled backward into Drew, who hauled him up and dragged him to the circle just as it exploded into a pile of ichor, leaving a small crater in the sand where Bash had been.

"I do not approve of that man for you," Thomas sneered.

The gash on her leg burned and throbbed, but she stood upright. "Leave him alone. This is about us."

"You're right. I want this to be my new home." Adira sidled up next to Thomas and he scratched her ears. "You can roll out the welcome mat now or I'll take you to my current apartment and we can talk about it there. I don't have running water though."

He cast a stream of electricity at Laura, and she repelled it with a small firewall, sending it back to him with a jolt.

"Patricide is a major sin, honey."

"If I'm already condemned, why should I care?" She scooped her hands, and a torrent of flame pushed him flying into the rocks.

"You've been practicing." While Thomas gathered himself, the dog snapped its jaws and Adira poised to strike.

He gave a sharp whistle and the dog charged. Laura landed a fireball just close enough to stop him and then Adira sprang at her. Bash shot at the big cat's feet, and she wheeled on him, rebounding off the force of his shield.

Her voice echoed in his head, "Do not fire on me, you stupid man."

Bash yelped and covered his ears. "Someone could have mentioned that!"

Drew blinked at him. "How did you *think* a mountain lion was talking to us?"

Thomas fired a band of power into Bash and though it drove him to the ground, Laura's protections again limited the force of his blast.

"You're getting stronger all the time," Thomas said to her as he swung his arm wide, heaving her into the sand and snuffing out her flames, "but, you're still just a baby."

He straightened his jacket. "Speaking of babies," At the wave of his hand, Brian slid down the embankment and stood next to him. "I knew if I was patient, I would get the son I always wanted."

Laura sat back on her heels. "Brian?"

As he filled his palms with emerald threads of light, Brian cast his glance from Thomas to Laura.

His mother's features hardened and for the first time ever her face was impossible to read. He hoped she'd be able to forgive him someday.

Drew ordered Audi into the circle after she pounded the last stake, and she took a knee in front of the cord Sarah had set to a slow burn between the candles. All of Sarah's powers were focused on the spell and on shutting out the banshee's hysterical screams.

The Bobs flanked Bash and Drew, but they didn't attempt a fresh attack. "Mom, I think it's working."

Bash spoke low in Sarah's ear. "It's midnight. What's happening?"

She pressed her hands to her temples. "Almost."

Laura rose to standing as Thomas taunted her with Brian's betrayal. "How powerful could you really be if you don't even know your own child?"

She smiled, "I could ask you the same question."

When Brian called her the night before to confess his abilities and his meetings with Thomas, she'd been genuinely furious. Not that he had powers, but that she'd allowed herself to be so blind to them. She was furious that he didn't trust her with the knowledge, and furious that she'd given him no reason to do so. They'd argued and cried and then against every protective maternal instinct she had, they made a plan to work together.

"Mom," Brian said.

She held her hand out to him, and he stepped away from Thomas.

"Catch." Brian tossed her the lightning, and she hurled it at the nearest tent stake. Brian dove inside the circle just before the power connected each metal spike, forming a solid pentacle of protection around Laura's loved ones.

Audi slapped his back. "You're so grounded."

Thomas roared in frustration and exchanged bolts of force with his daughter. Though pain wracked her body with each shock, she could sense his energy fading as the night waned. She clapped her hands together and the earth shook beneath them, knocking him off balance.

Sarah jumped up as, at last, the cord burned through the blood magic. "Adira?"

Her spell had released his hold over them and all of the cats made a dash for the rocks above.

"Brat!" Furious at Sarah, Thomas spun wildly and threw lightning at the ridge, causing a landslide that sent Rueben tumbling to the bottom of the canyon.

Laura flicked her nails again and pitched a static coated bomb at Thomas' chest. Sarah left the circle for Laura's side, combining their forces to drive him back to the edge of his gate.

As they closed on him, he grabbed hold of Laura and pulled her off her feet.

Bash lunged for the edge of the circle, but Daniel appeared and shoved him back. "He will take you both, and *you* will not survive the trip."

"I don't care!" Bash shouted and struggled against him.

Daniel held him fast and Drew begged, "Why won't you help us?"

Thomas spat in Daniel's direction and gasped. "You have no power over me, brother. There's nothing you can do."

"Don't let up!" Laura shouted at Sarah and scratched at the sand to get free. Then the dog latched his jaws onto her shirt, holding her steady enough to get one last shot at Thomas. As it hit, he slid into the gate and Adira leapt from the rocks above, her teeth tearing into the flesh at his neck as the weight of her body drove them both into the dusty void.

Daniel released Bash. "I'm going after her." He tossed Drew another smooth black stone. "If I don't return, use this to seal it."

Brian peered into the gate after Daniel. "Who the hell was that?"

Blistered and smoking, Daniel surfaced a few moments later dragging Adira by the scruff of her neck. She snapped her jaws at him as he released her, but he grabbed her head and growled in her ear, "Lions do not scare me anymore."

Then he yelled for Drew, "Do it now!"

Drew hurled the stone into the gate, sealing it in a ring of ice. Audi chucked her hammer after it and the gate shattered in a million pieces.

## *Chapter Twenty-Four*

Sarah sprinted to where Rueben's body lay half-buried in rubble and surrounded by dead goblins. Bash searched in a panic until he found Chuck and Isaac nearby. Chuck was already on the phone with emergency medical services.

Sarah flew at Daniel. "Bring him back!"

His eyes softened with compassion, but he could not do what she asked. "That's not how it works, Sarah. Thomas is right. My powers are specific to certain needs."

The rest of them sank to their knees and shoveled the dirt away from Rueben.

Drew's face twisted with fury. "Your god is just playing with us."

It is not a game, Andrew. It's a war on many fronts and there will be casualties.

Laura threw a pile of rocks to the side. "We didn't choose to be born and no one here chose to fight for you."

"No, you didn't. You're all just orphans, widowed, abandoned, and abused. Yet, you came together, determined to make miracles on your own." He knelt and smoothed the dirt from Rueben's face. "Of course you didn't choose this life, Laura. You were chosen for it."

* * *

After the funeral, Sarah stood rigid near Rueben's grave. It never occurred to her that the banshee screamed for her husband. Knowing that it would have been harder to live without Laura than Rueben sent pangs of guilt rippling through her conscience. Her married life was lonely and complicated but at one time she had truly loved him and it would be a lie to say that she wasn't frightened by the future.

Near the cemetery wall, Sebastian found Andrew leaning against a cottonwood tree, watching Sarah.

"Don't take this on, friend. You didn't wish for it."

Drew shoved his hands in his pockets. "What if subconsciously I did?"

"Shut up. A heart like yours is not even capable of that."

"I've never understood the human rush to self-judgment." Daniel appeared from behind the wall, startling them both.

Bash clenched his fists and said, "I'm getting you a bell."

"Believe me, Andrew," Daniel counseled him, "the judgment department is fully staffed."

At Brona's grave, the dog stood next to Laura as she wondered if she would ever know who her mother was. Contemplating the vase she'd kicked over before, she realized there could be no forgiveness and if she knew the whole of Brona's story, it would probably frustrate her even more.

For a while she'd thought that if she could understand why, then she could heal. But the woman did what she did and the 'why' was not important. Without shedding a single tear, Laura righted the vase and left to find her sister.

Daniel was busy herding everyone toward the Cottonwood tree when Laura approached.

Bash crouched to nuzzle the dog's neck and looked up at her. "Have you decided on a name?" Once freed from Thomas, the young German Shepherd hadn't left her side.

"I like Watson."

Daniel gave her a knowing smile before sobering his tone. "There's a shift coming, and I know you've felt it. Things are waking up. Old things, dirty things and beings that will take advantage as humanity regresses. Earth is a sacred place in the universe and there are extraordinary forces that resent your hold over her. As she changes under your watch, there will be a war for dominance and goblins will be the least of your worries. You can also rest assured that Thomas will want to be right in the middle of it."

Laura knelt beside Bash and Watson and said sadly, "He told me of this war."

Daniel stroked her hair, and that time she felt a small sensation of comfort at his touch. "You're dangerous and unpredictable and I still have my concerns. I believe I've deciphered your moral code though, such as it is, and there's no questioning your resolve." He gestured to the others, "The family you've built is exceptional."

Laura was doubtful. "Does this mean we've been forgiven?"

"Ha," Sarah muttered under her breath, "for being born?"

"No, Sarah," Daniel gave Watson a pat on the head and looked to the sky. "You've been drafted."

## *About the Author*

Vanessa Haney grew up in rural Arizona with, tragically, no access to the Other Side. Had there been a portal, she would have gone through it a long time ago. Instead, she makes a happy life in less rural Arizona with her son Connor, her partner Mike and two black cats named Shadow and Felix. There she writes, hikes and watches way too many horror movies.

Sign up to follow her adventures at:
http://www.vanessahaneywrites.com